These Worn Bodies

flash fiction

Avitus B. Carle

moon city press
Department of English
Missouri State University

The 2023 Moon City Short Fiction Award

MOON CITY PRESS
Department of English
Missouri State University
901 South National Avenue
Springfield, Missouri 65897
www.moon-city-press.com

The stories contained herein are works of fiction. All incidents, situations, institutions, governments, and people are fictional, and any similarity to characters or persons living or dead is strictly coincidental.

First Edition
Copyright © 2024 by Avitus B. Carle
All rights reserved.
Published by Moon City Press, Springfield, Missouri, USA, in 2024.
Manufactured in the United States of America.

Library of Congress Cataloging-in-Publication Data

Library of Congress Control Number: 2024948918
Carle, Avitus B., 1990-
These Worn Bodies

Further Library of Congress information is available upon request.

ISBN-10: 0-913785-79-9
ISBN-13: 978-0-913785-79-9

Cover designed by Shen Chen Hsieh
Interior designed by Katelyn Thornton
Text edited by Karen Craigo
Author photo by Ashley Alliano

moon city press
Department of English
Missouri State University

Contents

For Mom and Dad

These Worn Bodies

flash fiction

Bite

We open our mouths. Drop our bullets on our tongues. Taste the metal and three of us cough up powder. One of us nods. All of us nod. And we bite. We bite our bullets with our back teeth, listen to the sounds of our sprouting bones cracking within our gums. We bite to strengthen our jaws. We bite to quiet our laughter. We bite to practice how to warp our words, how to tuck them within our bullets. We are girls in lace cradling bullets in our palms. Bullets stolen from our fathers' guns, from their safes; souvenir bullets our grandfathers kept from the wars they relive in their sleep. We remember the stories of our grandmothers and mothers and wonder where their bullets are now. Two of us turn away from the circle, take aim at their targets in the distance. Four of us turn. Seven. Ten, taking aim with puckered lips. We aim at those who tell us to *hush.* At those who tell us to be good little girls. Pretty little girls. Silent and still little girls. All at once, we fire. We fire like our grandmothers and mothers. We fire our bullets encased in our words and wait for the sounds of impact.

My Brother Scarecrow

I'm six years old when I find the bodies of my parents stuffed inside one of my grandmother's trunks in the attic. I scream because their eyes are black buttons, because I can still recognize them even though their heads are made with sacks that read "potatoes" and "grain." I lose my voice somewhere in the attic that day before my grandma finds me, takes me in her arms, and scratches my back.

She tells me to *hush*. That they are just scarecrows. I still don't understand because there are no crows to scare in the attic. *No baby*, she says, *no*. My grandma reaches into the trunk and grasps my mother's hand. Some straw slips out and I reach to grab it but change my mind halfway through. I look to see if my grandma notices but her eyes are wet and sagging more than usual and the lines going down her neck like railroad tracks are moving like the strings of my cello.

"Hey, baby," she says to the body of my mother. My mother, the scarecrow, who has a mouth made of purple felt triangles.

"Let's take them out," I say because that's what I think my grandma wants.

But she closes the trunk instead.

"No, not them," and she carries my body to another trunk. "Try him."

Inside the trunk my grandma lets me open, dressed in a sailor's uniform and hat, is the body of my brother.

My mom and dad told me they'd be back soon. They kissed my head, made me promise to be good. I heard my mom whisper to grandma *Just three days, promise.*

Then, they left.

It's why she keeps their bodies in the attic, *Gone but not gone,* she says.

My brother is different because he died before I can remember. Grandma says I should still get to know him, so we take him outside, stretch his arms across a post and wrap his legs in a twist at the bottom.

"So he won't fall," grandma says.

To me, it looks like he's going to take off, legs untwisting like a pinwheel or propeller. When Grandma goes back inside to make dinner, I pretend to fly circles around my brother, practicing for when he's ready to take off.

My grandma teaches me how to make scarecrows, how to change and mend my brother's limbs. While we wrap a scarf around his neck before winter hits, my grandma tells me the truth. That my brother was born years before me, when my parents were tenderhearted teens. A boy who laughed, mostly to himself. A Navy man because he loved the ocean, a body somewhere in the depths of the sea.

I step back and stare at my brother who is still taller than me even without his pole. Think about how we're still both here. But he's the one made of straw wearing one of our father's throwaway coats and pants. With a flat-line mouth stitched from red thread and chipped, brown, button eyes.

Yet, I'm the one my parents left behind.

I stop visiting my brother after that.

I get the call that my grandma has died when I'm twenty-five and grass blades start stealing frost overnight. I have a boyfriend who I might marry and a girlfriend I could marry and question which I should tell or ask to come home with me. Though I know this is my chance to tell both about the other, to soften the blow because I'm grieving and selfish, I turn off my phone and drive home alone.

But halfway there I remember: my brother.

A neighbor tells me he found my grandma taking a nap at my brother's feet. Though, instead of my brother he says, *that dang scarecrow*, and that my grandma wasn't actually napping. She was still there in the evening, with ants and beetles in her hair. Mouth cocked open, he says, *like she had something important she wanted to say.*

I thank him, I don't know why, and he leaves me alone with my brother. My brother, in his scarf, sailor's hat, and our father's throwaway things. Legs still wound like a propeller. I take him down, his large body folds over my shoulder. *Still taller than me*, I tell him where I think his ear might be, and we go inside.

I put him on my grandma's chair, pass him yesterday's newspaper to read, then check on the bodies of my parents in the attic. The trunk is closed, I can see that before I'm all the way up, but my mother's hand lays limp outside it. I hold her hand and search for my grandma but the cloth is cold in my grasp. Inside the trunk are my parents' bodies, still folded into one another. I don't apologize to my mother for stealing her hand, slamming the trunk closed. I take it along with my grandma's spare materials, sit in the living room with my brother. I sew a face with sunflower button eyes, a crooked something I'm too embarrassed to call a smile or mouth. A long-sleeved orange dress with a white apron on top, and a hat made of straw with a green ribbon wrapped around.

When she is ready, I escort the body of my grandmother outside.

She lounges on the pole, one hand raised, green ribbon blowing in the breeze. I take my mother's severed hand, watch bits of straw escape from the bottom and elope with helicopter seeds. I place her hand in the pocket of my grandma's apron, step away and stare at what I've done.

My crooked-mouth grandma, with sunflower eyes and orange dress blowing in the wind revealing just enough of her legs to be scandalous. Knowing, or not, that the severed hand of her daughter waves to those who pass as her grandson laughs to himself while turning the page of yesterday's paper

So Many Clowns

To the Nail Polish Manufacturer,

I am writing to express my deepest disappointment in your nail polish entitled "So Many Clowns." Though I found the bronze tone of the nail polish beautiful, and the added sheen and nail strengthener a pleasant surprise, your polish did not induce the visions of multiple clowns as advertised.

I purchased your product with my husband in mind. On our first date, he took me to the circus and promptly abandoned me in the stands. You can imagine my disappointment, being stood up on a date surrounded by children, cotton candy, and parents drowning their misery in overly salted, buttered popcorn. I had it in my head to pretend I was one of them—a miserable parent—whose child had spent the entirety of the show being preoccupied in the bathroom. I even started planning my rant to the ringmaster and how his foul cotton candy preyed upon the stomach of my imaginary child.

But then a clown took center stage.

He had a blue nose that whistled instead of honked, red hair and patchwork clothes that made him look like a ragdoll. He was attempting to set the table but everything kept going wrong. The tablecloth got stuck in the zipper of his pants, causing all the dishes to fall when he moved to retrieve a second chair. When trying to light the wick of his two candles, either his nose or hair caught on fire and, the poor clown's flowers that were meant to be his centerpiece, were either too tall or too short for the vase.

And, despite being abandoned at the circus, I laughed.

His act ended when he set two whipped cream pies on either side of the table. Then, to my and the audience's surprise, he started searching for his date. You can imagine how many children wanted to join him but I was surprised by how many men and women who raised their hands as well. Out of all those people, his hand stretched out toward the spotlight which was squarely focused on me.

I don't know what moved me to join him, probably the fact that I was meant to be on a date anyway. I took that clown's hand and he had the nerve to say, *Sorry I took so long*. I was shocked to recognize the voice of my date, the man who'd abandoned me, coming out of this clown! We took our seats, he gestured for me to try the pie, and I decided to throw it in his face instead.

The audience laughed and I laughed because, apparently, I had thrown the pie with such force that he was thrown back in his chair, taking the silverware, uneven flowers, and table settings with him. I've never laughed so hard in my life, making two more decisions in that moment. One, to kiss this clown on his whipped-cream-covered cheek, and two, that he would be the man I married.

He died just after four years of marriage. I later learned a clown can only cheat death by fire so many times and that it was one of many occupational hazards of clowning. I was hoping that, out of all the clowns your product promises to reveal, one of them might be him.

I painted So Many Clowns onto my fingernails and toenails, slept beside the open bottle for three nights in a row, and even shared it with some of my husband's former coworkers. I was shocked to learn that, out of all their years in clowning, that they have never used nor have they even heard of your particular brand of nail polish. In a final attempt to induce the vision of multiple clowns, I inhaled your product, five times per nostril for good measure. I am frustrated to report that I walked away with a severe migraine and not a single clown sighting. Either rename your nail polish "Bronze Shield Guard," or remove it from your shelves entirely.

And, rest assured, I will be warning other members of the clown community and the widowed clowning society about your nail polish.

Gentlemen Callers

I find my boyfriend's car parked in front of the Hillside Motel and consider shattering the windows or, at least, peeing on the windshield. But that's bad for business. Not my business because, technically, he's my ex-boyfriend and, fortunately, it's my grandmother's 80th birthday.

She deserves a granddaughter who can behave, who can do as she's told, even though I'm neither of those things. Instead of being here at 5 p.m. like she asked, I'm in front of her usual room at 4.

Instead of carrot ccake in a white box, I have a red velvet in a pink box because I don't like carrot cake, and she knows I don't, just like she probably knows that my ex shouldn't be one of her gentlemen callers.

That's what my mother calls them. Ever since "sperm donor" was revealed to be an inappropriate way for me to introduce my grandfather to my second-grade class.

Her gentlemen callers used to come to the house until my 12-year-old self caught one climbing through my window. My grandmother would later describe him as a man who had "a thing for breaking and entering," with a wink that haunts me to this day. Then came the motels, though she's settled on room 28 at the Hillside Motel 5 miles from our house.

I told my ex all this in the car that's now parked outside my grandmother's room. Same car he parked outside of our house, when he first met my mother and Ethel. I didn't feel anything when my grandmother and he talked about football all night, him sitting next to her and across from me at dinner. Her reapplying her lipstick in the mirror, him licking his lips and talking about her delicious pie. How excited he was to dive in, to taste, already ready for seconds and thirds.

I didn't start feeling anything until I walked him back to his car, expecting to be invited somewhere, but he starts talking about my grandma and how she "gets" him like I don't, but, just in case, I tell him I do. I do get him, and he says something about needing space and things will be better this way and something about meeting someone else.

"Oh," and this he says after braking too hard, after I start thinking he's changed his mind, "let Ethel know, if she needs anyone to taste-test her pies, I'm free."

Maybe this shit-covered bench and melting red velvet cake and I all deserve each other. A man, not my ex, walks out of room 28. Between him zipping his pants and the cool air that escapes from the room, I can see my grandmother's legs rocking. The mole on my ex's ass like a dab of ink.

"Oh," the man stares at me. His lip twitches as the door closes. "You must be—"

"Don't." It's weird when they acknowledge me. Worse when they say I look just like Ethel, them smelling like Vicks, my grandmother's cure-all.

I'm not sure how much time passes. Only that I can see my grandmother's hand between the curtains. The fog of her breath. She's really into whatever my ex is doing to her, and I try not to be jealous, but Ethel doesn't work up a fog for just anyone, and I can't help but wonder why he never did anything, like he's doing to her, to me.

A Jeep pulls into the lot and parks in front of my grandmother's room. A not-hideous guy with red curls and freckles crossing his crooked nose almost falls out, pauses, and climbs back in to turn off the engine. He almost trips as he walks over, eyes the empty spot next to me on the bench before passing. I watch him, because my viewing options are limited, trace the numbers on the doors.

"Good day for 22," he says, and, at first, I don't realize he's talking to me. Why would he? All any guy around here wants is Ethel. Until he's sitting next to me, our knees touching, and he makes the same comment again.

"We don't have to talk."

His thumbs go to war with each other. "You here to see Ethel, too?"

Gross.

But maybe it's because he knows my grandmother's name instead of asking for mine or saying we look alike, or I remind him of her, or that he moves slightly closer for my answer like he's interested in what I have to say that I cough and almost drop the red velvet cake and sputter,

"No—yes, it's not—"

"Are you OK?"

He takes the cake because I'm choking on my spit. He pats my back, and I shake my head, which he must think means no, no, I'm not OK, which is true because my ex, the supposed-to-marry-and-have-kids-with ex, is one of my grandmother's gentlemen callers.

"I should ruin his car."

"Seems like a waste of cake." The red-haired guy smiles, stretching his freckles, and it's almost sweet that he thinks I mean to use the cake as my weapon of destruction.

And, rather than think about how unfair all this is, I remove the lid from the cake. I sink my hand into its center and am surprised that the guy remains still, balancing the cake on his lap.

And I eat. I shovel red velvet chunks into my mouth until it's full. Until I'm pushing red velvet chunks into his mouth, and he's shy at first, pulling away until he tastes my fingers and begs for more. His face and neck turn red with cake, or blush, I don't know, and I don't care because, on that shit-covered bench, we feed each other and lick the leftovers from each other's fingers, and through it all, I can see his lips move, and the sound of a door opening escapes and someone asks, "How does it taste?"

"Delicious."

How We Survive

We survive on vegetables from gardens we make in the backyards of strangers.

Blasting music with all the windows open, raiding closets, setting food bowls on porches just in case our tabby, rottweiler, ferret, hamster, or goldfish comes home.

We are the last people on Earth.

You say this every night before you go to your room and I go to mine in a house that was never ours.

We survive on secrets.

Over breakfast I admit that sometimes I wish you'd come to my room. You say you wish you'd known sooner. That you've met someone and wasn't sure when to tell me. I try to remember all the times we've been apart, wonder how you managed to meet someone when we are the last people on Earth.

I want you to meet her, you say, and I nod because I don't know what else to do.

We survive on a series of miscommunications.

You take me to the nearby sex shop and tell me her name's Lorraine. I look for evidence of another human, someone I could be friends with. Someone I could envy, address hateful letters to that I'll never send but burn in the firepit while you sleep. Someone I could have rebound sex with—to stop pretending like you and I have ever had sex. I start building a life with this woman you've met named Lorraine.

You walk to the display window (I take a moment to admire your ass and think maybe I have a chance) and carry a mannequin towards me.

Meet Lorraine, you say.

We survive on fuck-ups and moments of doubt.

Like how did I fuck up this badly? How did you fuck a—Lorraine?

Lorraine has blue hair and eyes that never shut. She's wearing a black latex catsuit that accentuates her hips and legs in a way I can't hate and is made of fucking plaster.

Don't embarrass me, you hiss.

I shake her hand. *Nice to meet you*, I say, while thinking about all the things I didn't do that drove you to Lorraine.

We survive on privacy.

Lorraine starts coming home with you after we meet, and I hear you two through the walls. You tell her about your life before we were the last people on Earth, and everyone you miss. I hear you two having sex when I'm trying to sleep. Sometimes, I hear my door creak open and think you've come to apologize. Instead, I see Lorraine, leaning in the doorframe, naked and frozen in her shop-window pose.

We survive on new experiences.

You ask me to move out. Say, it's nothing personal, just that you and Lorraine need your privacy. I consider telling you about Lorraine in my doorway but you're babbling about how new everything is with her. You hear birds singing (there are none), music playing (you keep Rick-rolling me), and everything is so much brighter. It's not. It's not because, since we're the last people on Earth, everything is still the same.

We survive on small moments.

Since being evicted, I've decided to house-hop. I want to find this brightness—or newness—you've found so I migrate from one house to the next. Somehow you find me, and I think I feel a little bit of that brightness you've found.

Lorraine's throwing a party, you say, and hand me an invitation.

I invite you inside. You back away.

Sorry, Lorraine's waiting.

We survive on disappointments.

I find a dress in someone's basement that fits and heels that I hope I can walk in. Your house is somehow crowded by the time I arrive. Lorraine is wearing a pink tutu over a red leather catsuit, and she's surrounded by other mannequins I recognize from various department stores and sex shops. Even the one from the auto body shop is here. I make my way over to him and try to start a conversation, but he doesn't respond, so I lean against him and imagine our lives together.

We survive on possibilities.

My husband—the mannequin from the auto body shop—would address me as his partner instead of wife. He would take my last name, never comment on my age, how many pills I take, the diapers I'll eventually need. He'd hold my hand, kiss me often, and tell me how much he loves me. He'd tell me he loves me so often that I'd forget about the party, Lorraine, and you asking Lorraine to marry you.

We survive on the promise of the future.

You invite me to the wedding, and I come. Lorraine wears a white pantsuit and you—a wedding gown. The mannequin from the auto body shop is there, but he sits far away from me. You whisper your vows, kiss Lorraine, and announce that you are now Mr. Lorraine. You thank everyone for coming. You thank me for coming. I have a few drinks and make my way to the backyard. You find me, like you always do, and ask if you can have a taste.

We survive on missed opportunities.

You ask why we—I tell you I don't know. That's a lie, but you've had one too many, and this conversation seems inappropriate on your wedding night. I tell you I'm leaving, and you tell me you know. You say you've noticed all the times I've moved, each time farther away from you; how I flirted with the guy from the auto body shop only to now pretend he doesn't exist.

I tell you I think you're beautiful. Handsome. That I don't know which you would prefer.

I guess that's why we never—

I press my finger to your lips. You're crying, which shouldn't be happening. I look for Lorraine. You grab my hand and I know, if you asked me to stay, my answer would destroy everything.

The Waitress Draws a Ketchup Heart Within the Mouth of a Denny's Platter

Abandons it with the boy playing with her parents, the boy forbidden to call her "Mom."

The Science
of Saying Goodbye

Before:

1.   Mama covers the house with pillow cotton filling she buys from Etsy and Target. When I ask her why, she doesn't respond, just prints out articles filled with words I don't understand with titles that include "The Science of Clouds," "How to Soften the Blow," and "Preparing to Saying Goodbye."

2.   A bed appears in the living room the same day my mother burns all the pictures of my father. I witness her draggin a match where my father's photographic spine would be, the flame snacking on my father's center. My mother drops the picture in the trash before the flame tastes my father's smile. Before it can taste the image of me in midair, either freshly released from my father's grasp or waiting to return.

3.   My mother challenges me to a pillow fight and swats me like a wasp, quick enough to catch me off guard and again to make sure I don't have time to rebel. She uses the pillows form the metal bed that floats on shredded cotton, the one in our living room facing the

TV. We jump on the bed, swinging our pillows, until our heads tap against the ceiling. My mother jumps into the clouds, pretends her pillow is her parachute, and I follow her into the soft, cotton mist. When I land, my mother wraps her arms around me, and I think she's kissing her love for me into my hair. However, when she pulls away, she whispers someone else's name, not mine. *Joyce.*

During:

1.   Three men carry a woman made of paper and bone and place her on the metal bed. My mother is on her like the ants to the honey trail I made last summer, hoping they would be the keepers of the secrets I once shared with my father. My mother wrings a damp towel over the woman's lips and I watch them unfurl like petals.

2.   I learn that the woman's name is Joyce and that she is my aunt. When she talks, I hear her skin rustle like birds and squirrels in the bushes. *I remember you.* My aunt Joyce grabs my arm, shatters her face with a smile. *There's a snake constricting my heart,* and she presses my head to her chest. I hear the sounds of her heart gasp, the whistle of her breath escaping from her nose. I never hear the snake in her chest, though I see it slither beneath the skin of her neck when she swallows.

3.   My mother warns that aunt Joyce is not a toy even though my aunt asks me to braid the clouds into her hair like one of my dolls. *So I can fly*, she says, as I tuck cotton balls around her edges like a crown , every time I try to braid my doll's hair, my fingers end up in knots.

4.   Aunt Joyce dances in the clouds with a suffocated red balloon dangling from her mouth. I've never seen

her walk before—didn't even know she could. *Dance with me, child,* and before I can answer, she pulls me by my hand. We kick up the clouds, sing the songs my aunt makes up. I don't know when my aunt becomes my mother, calling me baby, child, baby. I age five different times as they spin me around the room, until the clouds swallow the metal bed and tickle the red balloon.

5. My aunt turns to paper for four days, confined to the metal bed. My mother asks that I leave aunt Joyce alone but, at night, I climb up to visit her. I knead the skin covering her cheeks, searching for myself, my mother, the dancing woman, the one with the red balloon.

6. *Your father was a snake.* Before I can ask my aunt how she knows, she returns to being paper. I clear the cotton clouds from around her bed, try to find her red balloon. At night, I watch an invisible force tug on my aunt's chest, forcing it to rise, before letting it fall again. I wait for the snake, for my father to come, hoping my aunt and he are willing to share their secrets with me.

7. A man wraps a white sheet around Aunt Joyce and carries her away. My mother is in the doorway biting the skin from her thumb and licking her tears. My father must have come sometime in the night and disliked what he saw.

After:

1. My mother grabs a knife and slices the metal bed's mattress. The mattress spits up feathers and I think it's crying for help. When the mattress is nothing but cloth, I wrap my arms around my mother's fallen body. *Baby,* she calls me and I tell her I'm here, and this time, she knows my name.

2.   When I tell her about my father being a snake, my mother says it's true. I ask if he took Aunt Joyce away. *He'd have to be here to do that.* Every word she spits lands on my face, my skin soaking them in like antivenin.

3.   After we clear the clouds away and after the metal frame is gone, my mother goes to bed. I stare at my reflection, my throat, in the mirror, making sure the snake isn't there. I tell myself to go to bed, then I feel something nudge the back of my head. Aunt Joyce's red balloon, still dancing above the ground, floats past me and taps the window. I hug the balloon to my chest, thinking this is how I'll bring her back. Aunt Joyce must have tucked her breath into this balloon, so my father wouldn't steal all of her. I open the door and the balloon wiggles free, the last bit of Aunt Joyce floating towards the clouds. *It's what she wanted,* someone says, and I think how unfair the whole thing is. Especially since nobody ever asked about me.

Subject: Where's Your Second Novel and All the Subsequent Drafts I Reply

In the queue waiting to print. In my printer, waiting for me to get more ink. In your inbox. Check your spam folder. Folded into hundreds of paper frogs, each reading the A*dventures of Frog and Toad* or humming excerpts from *The Rainbow Connection*. I can't work under these conditions. I can't write while my novel frogs taunt me, spitting my words at dead flies on the windowsill. My wife thinks I should take a break, collect my thoughts. She places my manuscript—the one with all your notes on green Post-it slivers—in her bedside drawer, and by morning the whole things transformed into frogs. She rubs my back, says I'm stressed, I'm seeing things, says there's nothing there. I interrupt her, ask if she's read my manuscript, so it sounds like her response to my question is *There's nothing there.* I start from scratch. The frogs hibernate. I start with "the." I begin at the end, middle, with the death of the main character. I admit that I am an imposter. The frogs come back. They take over my office, it would be rude to kick them out of their home. I go for a walk with my wife. I let the frogs type responses to your email, all of which I delete. The frogs only know the words in my novel. My wife asks me to tell her a story, not the one due to you, but one off the top of my head. I remember my grandfather balancing on lily pads and mocking snakes with his tongue. My wife wants me to write that story instead. The frogs do, too; they have invaded our bedroom, though my wife still can't see them. The frogs exit out of Word while I try to apply your edits. Hop on delete, backspace, every time I try to save, they hop on enter, selecting no. I shred the frogs at Staples. Witness my words become so small, a child grabs them in her fists, throws them, and names my novel *Snow*. I cry on the couch. I cry with my head resting on my wife's lap. She promises everything will be OK, that I just need more time. I think about asking for more time, another extension, a chance to start a new project. I sleep in the farthest spaces from my computer, from you, from your email. My wife wants to go on a walk, says she forgot her wallet on her bedside table. Before I can grab it, I hear the chirpings of frogs. I wrap my hands around them and take them to my office. We settle in front of my computer, these new frogs and I, and I listen to them croak the names I'd forgotten. The truth about my grandfather, those lily pads, and snakes. Together, we write everything down, until I hear my wife laugh from behind. She's not mad about the walk, though she's concerned about the frogs, but hopefully, she'll understand. I hope you understand, I'm not sorry this took so long.

Please see attached and sorry about the mucus. You know how frogs are.

How to Fail a Job Interview or Why You're the Only Wannabe Librarian Here

Tell your future employer you're sorry for being late. Your phone died. The funeral was lovely, a very private affair. Just you, your neighbor—who stopped by to say a few words on his way to the mailbox—and your son. You buried your phone in a Converse shoebox in the backyard, thanked her for all her years of service while sprinkling rice into the open grave. Your son—a rude and unthinking man—offered to buy you a new phone before you could throw the first clump of dirt, so of course, you had to take a moment to explain the etiquette that is expected of him at a funeral.

Tell her you pressed your blouse underneath your mattress because who irons anymore? Sure, the left sleeve is wrinkled, and the collar is wrinkled and there are two, three, five buttons missing. But would she have even noticed that your blouse is being held together by safety pins if you hadn't told her? Remind your future employer that this is a show of commitment. An attestation to your ingenuity.

Tell her that, after you left your house, you stopped by Manhattan Bagel. Ordered a sausage, egg, and cheese breakfast sandwich because your son refused to eat with you. After the funeral, you'd invited him inside. Turned the stove on and got your best pan because he loves scrambled eggs. He tells you he's good right after you put the butter in, right after you tell him you have good news and after he loans you his personal cellphone because he can just use his work phone for now. You told the Manhattan Bagel cashier your good news—that you have a job interview today—not that he asked but someone other than you should know since your son didn't ask and couldn't find the time to stay for scrambled eggs.

Tell her how you never cared for scrambled or powdered eggs, though your son swears they're "not that bad" like so many things he's tried to introduce you to. Talk over the interviewer, apologize for interrupting, but keep talking anyway. Hand her your resume. Slip in the fact that you are over 50 because—though not obvious—she'll probably ask why you left the year off your birthday. Admit that you are closer to 60, which isn't a lie, since you look pretty good for 72.

Tell her that, after you finished eating, you found the building and were appalled to find all these employees behind glass like wax figures in a museum. And out of everyone, you're the only one with gray hair. Not now, of course, since you had your roots touched up for this interview, but what does that say about the library's culture? Not a single person pushing 60? Not that you want to be surrounded by the kinds of people who eat powdered eggs and complain about arthritis and hearing loss and their knees giving out. Apologize to the interviewer. Tell her your son said some things after you turned the stove on. That he worries, that all children worry about their parents, but the interviewer shouldn't worry about you. You know you're an upstanding citizen, but it's unfair for this job to expect you to represent an entire generation.

Tell her—now that you're here—you're wondering if this is the right opportunity for you. There were other interviews that you thought went well until everyone kept telling you no. One job was honest, said the company wanted someone younger on the team. Tell her that's how you lost your job of thirty years. To someone younger who could smile with ease, run up the stairs, and remember how to format spreadsheets so the columns populated information automatically. Assure the interviewer that you never wanted to stop working, never wanted to retire, but you appreciated the honesty of the company in their choice of someone younger.

Ask her if she remembers the last thing she said to her parents. Not on the phone, to their faces. Miss the interviewer's response because you are thinking about your son. How you misheard "nursing" as "nursery" though you think these are just bookends for a life. Ask if you look like someone who needs nursing. That's why you were appalled by this building_too many windows, both inside and out. The employees remind you of wax figures with their plastered smiles. Nobody likes wax figures or would want one in their house which is why you only ever see them behind glass—same as the people on the brochure you threw in the pan with all that wasted butter.

Tell her to look at you—really look at you—and ask if all librarians are this stressed? That you wanted something to occupy your time, get you out of the house, perhaps create a scenario where you wouldn't be able to answer the phone after the first ring. So your son would see you aren't finished living yet. That you can take care of yourself, even if your memory slips from time to time.

Tell her never mind and stand before she has time to answer. You'll find a more suitable job in a building with fewer windows, both inside and out. You know the job market is terrible, but that doesn't mean you should stop trying. After all, you showed up here today and that says something about you.

Ignore whatever the interviewer is saying and check the phone your son loaned you. Notice several missed calls and texts that read CALL ME and laugh because it looks like your son is having a conversation with himself. Clutch the phone to your chest and consider telling the interviewer the importance of being needed. Change your mind. Thank your former future employer for her time and offer her your hand. Grasp her hand firmly and tell her, no, you don't want to open a savings account.

You are perfectly capable of saving yourself.

Sugar, Baby

I tell her I'm addicted to Sugar Babies. Not really, but that's all my daughter can handle. She doesn't ask what addicted means. Hell, she probably already knows. One time, she found an old spoon in my purse. I told her Mommy likes to collect old spoons. Next thing I know, she's collecting spoons, too. Plastic spoons that change color in water. Teaspoons she bends into rings. Spoons she leaves on the windowsill—mouth down—*to cook just like you,* she says. I don't know what to say, don't know when she saw me. I thought I was being careful. I tell her to stop collecting spoons and, of course, she asks me why. *'Cause it's bad*, I say, so she starts looking for something else to do. Kids have an eye for things, especially when it comes to keeping track of what their parents are doing. I wish I'd known that before the spoons. Definitely before the tinfoil. She makes a dog out of the tinfoil squares I hide in a tea box. Piglets from the squares she finds in plastic butter containers. Tinfoil birds takeoff from her piggy bank. In her piggy bank. This haunts me for weeks and I take a few Sugar Babies after I make sure she's sleeping. I tell myself, tomorrow, I'll tell her.

Tomorrow. Tomorrow. Today. I sit her on my knee, tell her about Sugar Babies. How they're not so good for me, that Mommy shouldn't have them anymore. I tell her I'm trying to stop. That I want today to be a good day. *What's a bad day,* she says, while playing connect the dots on the insides of my forearms. *Those are bad days,* I say, when mommy can't resist Sugar Babies. And I tell her it starts with one spoon. Starts with tinfoil and a need for more sugar, more of the soft chew filled with milk caramel, more than I can handle. Except that part's not true. I don't know if any of that's true. I don't know a lot because of these Sugar Babies I still have hidden behind the bottles of hot sauce her daddy loved. Even keep some tucked behind the box holding her daddy's ashes. The Sugar Babies took him, but I don't tell her that, just that I'm trying to make today a good day. *Some days are just bad,* she says, leaning into me. I tell her, yes, some days are, and her head cuddles into my bones and, maybe, I hear my skin start to tear. And though I told her that some days are bad, what I keep to myself is how few I have left.

Dandelion

The daisies remove their seedling shawls, use their leaves to unfurl tender white petals slick with dew. Whisper greetings to the sun, vying for his attention shown in the warm caress of his rays, before scoping out their new home. They were born of railroad soil, some blossoming amongst pebbles or between the grooves of footprints. Those who blossom close enough to the rails rest their heads upon chilled metal, their roots tingling from the chill.

Dandelion trembles from her place between wooden slats of railroad tracks, losing several of her seedling hairs in the wind. This bothers the daisies, some reaching to ensure their beautiful white petals remain attached to their yellow faces. All flowers know dandelions are common things, prone to play with unruly children with false promises of delivering wishes on the wind. Whose leaves claw at unwanted things and that they always travel in hordes, suffocating the innocent who are trying to make a home in freshly overturned soil. Why else would a flower sprout spikes if not to commit acts of murder?

Besides, only dandelions attract unwanted things.

Dandelion strains against her roots to gain the fleeting attentions of the daisies. When they continue to ignore her, Dandelion counts how many seedlings comprise her white Afro. Appearances are important to daisies and a bald Dandelion would be unsightly. Her sigh mixes with a gentle ping, one of her seedlings balancing on the rim of an inkwell, close enough for Dandelion to touch. She is sure the inkwell wasn't here yesterday. She shoos her seedling from the edge of the inkwell's lips, begins to ask if any of the Daisies might have misplaced it. But the inkwell glistens in the light, the scent of diesel oil rising from its center.

Since none of the daisies care about the inkwell, Dandelion decides to claim it for herself. At least, for the time being, since she is unsure of how long she has left between the railroad tracks. She apologizes for her appearance and constant shedding, her barbed leaves, and her overall lack of beauty. Dandelion doesn't believe she's ugly but knows she is not considered to be beautiful because the daisies remind her every blossoming season, which is also the reason they refuse to sprout anywhere near her.

The inkwell doesn't reply.

Because it's an inkwell and all sensible flowers know inkwells can't talk.

Dandelion giggles, twiddles her roots over her foolishness. She bends her stem to peer inside, gazes at the specks of glass puncturing holes in the dark. Dandelion remembers a time she was considered to be beautiful with wild strands of gold that honey bees loved to nap on. Weather and wind withered her roots, turning her yellow top into a puff ball that the Daisies can't stand to view. When one of her leaves caresses the insides of the inkwell, a smear of blue appears. Dandelion thinks the inkwell's beauty has perished due to years spent drinking oil.

Besides, only dandelions attract unwanted things.

Black Bottom Swamp Bottle Woman

Maybe you hear what they say. That you are the Black bottom woman. The Black swamp woman. The Black-hearted, Black-breasted, Black bottle woman. Maybe that suits you just fine, because maybe you deserve those names. Just like they, the people who come to your swamp and flick your lantern twice before leaving their bottles for you to clean, maybe they believe labeling and understanding mean the same thing.

Maybe, before you became the Black bottom, swamp bottle Black woman, you were just a Black woman. In a boat. In the swamp. Holding hands with a Black man who never asked you to marry him. Because, maybe, he was already married. Maybe he didn't love you enough to marry you, or maybe he did, and that's why he never asked. Maybe you never thought much about marriage because, maybe, you only thought about bottles. Talked to the Black man in the swamp on his boat about bottles. How to fill them, seal them, discard them.

Maybe the Black man didn't understand. Maybe he did and believed he could bear the weight of bottling and sealing. Maybe you find him in your bottling room. His eyes in Coke bottles. His lungs in water bottles. His heart beating in a bottle of pennies and his lips still talking in a model ship bottle, his secrets raising the sails.

Maybe your mama warns you about bottling and becoming the Black bottom swamp bottle woman. How there will always be someone who believes they know, but can't say for sure what it is that they know. Maybe, for your mama, that was a woman who sailed into the swamp on a canoe. Maybe your mama tells you how she borrowed the finger bone of this woman, soaked it in vinegar and jam and corn liquor. Let it sit in a bottle of castor oil and made you. And, maybe, this woman built ships in bottles until she made a ship that couldn't be bottled and, maybe, she asked your mama to join her and, maybe, your mama knew what she'd grow into without that woman. So, she left you to grow into that woman instead. Left you in the swamp with sunflowers and a series of *be goods* written on paper straw wrappers all slipped into bottles. Left you to listen for the people and their bottles filled with their secrets and memories and wants they don't want just like, maybe, you never wanted to be unwanted by the mama who made you. You, the Black bottom swamp bottle woman.

To All the Boys
We Never Kissed

What we had was never love. Affection. Infatuation. Lust. We are of an age where we can distinguish among them all just as we know the ways our lips can part. Not for you, but for them. For the boys we tried to love and those we did. For our husbands and lovers and boyfriends. Don't be sad; we remember you fondly. The boys with puckered lips while we leaned away. You, who had the courage to be honest, say, *I like you like you,* or *Maybe I could be that guy* whispered on porch steps. As we pumped our legs on the swing set, our velocities never synching. Spoken after we shared our misunderstandings of relationships and situationships and friends-with-benefits-ships and believing we were *the* girlfriend when, really, we weren't. You who listened to us.

And we laughed when you told us you loved us. Like your honesty was a joke. And we playfully punched your arms, slipped you into the friend zone as easily as we do with loose change into tip jars at our favorite coffee shops, unaware we couldn't afford to lose you. We are selfish in our ways of needing.

Selfish in our wanting and yes, we should have let you go. Should have been happy when you found someone who wants to be kissed by you instead of wondering why you stopped returning our calls or became busy with plans that no longer involved us. Why you hesitate to hug us. Why you say *Sorry, we can't do* that *anymore* like spending the day together or linking arms in public or you holding us as we cry about the guys we've hated to love is the problem when, we know, the person you text when you think we can't see, they are the problem.

Some of us learn how to be happy for you. For this new person you want to kiss. But some of us grow into our jealousy. We lurk in the virtual crevices of your social media feeds and wonder what do you see in our replacement? How their hips are too wide and their laugh is too loud and we'll remind you that, clearly, they're fake because no one is ever that happy. And we won't tell you we dream about plucking the hairs from their scalp, their unibrow, their mustache, their armpits, their legs, and imagine the moment you return to us and tell us how our replacement has changed. How you barely recognize them and we'll tell you we know and that we understand.

And you'll return to those of us who don't understand that you deserve to be happy, blinded by our love for you as a weapon to wield against the boys we've loved and wanted and kissed. You, on our arm, as we pass them by, pretending they are strangers to us. Until we turn the corner and you ask what's wrong, unaware even after all this time, that when we look at you, we are using you. To look to the boys we've kissed, to see if they've noticed how happy, carefree, and unbothered we seem. If, in the way their body moves when they walk farther away from us, if their eyes still search for us, if we've proven to the boys we've kissed that we will always have other options. To prove that, if we are still good enough for you, surely, we are good enough to be loved.

White Ribbons

My mother loses herself in the sounds of fingernail clicks and the dull thuds her forehead creates when colliding into the corners of our home. She dwells in these crevices where two walls meet, biting her lower lip until she bleeds. Releasing all the tension she carries throughout the day until the diaper she wears under her patchwork jeans overflows.

And she smiles.

Despite the smell. Despite me watching her, imagining the rapid clicks are a form of Morse code, a puzzle only I can decipher. A noise she makes just for me. I go to her, even though the smell of shit and lavender makes me cry. At least, this is what I keep in my mind as I wrap my arms around her waist and rest my chin on her shoulder.

"Tell me where you are," I whisper in the same voice she saved for scraped knees and bedtime stories.

"Birds mocking tales," she giggles through parted chapped lips revealing bloodstained teeth.

"Turn around," I say. All I want is for her to look at me, to acknowledge my presence in a world outside of her corner.

And, if our eyes meet, to ask her why she won't let me join her in a world of her creation.

The doctor says my mother has Alzheimer's, a word that I've learned starts with a sigh and gets caught on the "Z." I keep the word to myself, letting it linger in every sentence I'm supposed to say but hoard in my mind. When my mother becomes lost in one of her corners, I fill the quiet with the places she might be.

She is 12 with white ribbons braided into pigtails that rest just above her shoulders, the part cutting the surface of her scalp in half to reveal hazel skin. Toes send tidal waves along the surface of the lake where she watches her brother drown. She swallows her words for two years, believing that if a cry for help does nothing to save a life, what's the point in speaking. When she decides to speak again, she will always twist the story of her brother's death to match her mood or to gage the amount of emotional stress those around her can handle.

My mother loathes pity in all its forms.

She is 14 with a white ribbon twisting around her pointer finger, hazel skin her father loves, turning purple and cold. Toes send tidal waves along the surface of the lake where she watches him stand in the shallows, talking with bullfrogs and fireflies instead of going to work. She watches him go, carrying his brown leather suitcase with holes and handle patched with duct tape hanging from his side, beyond the screams of her mother followed by the clang of pots and pans crashing into walls and shattering windows. Beyond the lake, until she is left wondering why he left her behind amongst the sounds of the bullfrog songs he also claimed to love.

She is 18 watching a white ribbon float on the lake's surface, blades of grass scratching her hazel skin. She glances at her mother through the kitchen window every time the sun catches the glass, knowing her mother will keep on drinking until her anger feels fair, scream until there is nothing left but to face the darkness that awaits her. She watches her mother's shadow fade in the kitchen window, wonders how many steps her father took before he felt safe enough not to look back. She counts how many steps it takes to be free from her mother, not knowing that, even after her mother dies, the counting never stops.

She is 30 watching her baby play with a white ribbon in her fist, fingernails occasionally scratching her hazel skin. Sunlight punctures storm clouds, soaking them in raindrops large enough to create their own lakes and tidal waves, washing away what remains of her past. She thrives outdoors, listening to the sweet songs of cardinals and blue jays, her child matching the movements of her lips. Neither of them knowing she has already lived half her life.

"Tell me where you are," I ask again and this time she glances at me.

At least, this is what I hope for.

In the world I create for us, I am 4 years old. An age where I am able to speak while knowing the pleasures of being carried and napping in the warm crook of my mother's neck. She keeps stories of her brother from me, her father and mother becoming tender figures she models herself after. I ask her any question that comes to mind, fingers tracing her unchapped lips before cradling her hazel cheeks in my palms.

And she responds, not with fingernail clicks, but with arms that embrace me. Chokes the life out of songs by shattering the high notes and out-of-tune attempts to remember all the words. Who sees me. Hears me, and makes me believe that all the love is still there.

Without her voice.

Without her mind.

But this is not the world she has left me for.

Her teeth release her lip, gnashing with rage inside her cheeks. Her mouth quivers, body stiffening in my grasp. The clicks come in rapid succession sending signals I don't understand.

"Please," the words catch somewhere in my chest and everything I've hoarded threatens to come out at once but instead, I let them stir in my mind.

My mother has Alzheimer's and has forgotten my name. No, she's forgotten more than that. She is lost and I can't reach her because she no longer knows who I am, who I was, who we were. And, because of this, I can no longer find her.

"Tell me where you are," because I'm afraid to be without you.

Her lips part and, for a moment, I think my name somehow lingers on the edge, wanting to invite me in.

I Double-Dog Dare You

sleep with one eye open, pretend your brother doesn't prowl the halls at night, tell your mother he comes into your room, tell your teacher when she doesn't believe you, pick your cuticles until you bleed while waiting outside the principal's office, don't look at your mother as she snatches you by the arm, as she drags you home, as she sits you in front of your brother and makes him confess his love for you, makes him explain how much he loves you, start to believe that his form of love is natural, that you should have never spoken up in the first place, watch a romantic comedy to learn about love, watch the Hallmark Channel to learn about falling in love, watch movies and read books looking for the love you supposedly share with your brother, run away from home at 15 when you learn the words for what your brother does to you at night, go back after six months because you don't know how to take care of yourself, ignore the fact that your brother is waiting for you at the door, ignore him when he tells you that he missed you, that he knew you couldn't stay away, run away, for good this time, at 18 because you are an adult who can no longer take care of everyone else who would rather not take care of you, sleep with one eye open under bridges, make friends with a woman named Tulip, a former cleaning lady with a glass eye, tell Tulip about your brother, about your mother, cry in Tulip's arms when she believes every word you say even though she smells like metal and french fries, promise Tulip you'll get a job, that you won't let this define you, get a job at a diner with bubble-gum-colored chairs, fuck truck drivers in the alley for tips, don't tell Tulip about any of them, fall in-something with a truckdriver who buys you strawberry flavored Starbursts, travel cross country with said truck driver, write letters to Tulip, keep these letters in the Power Ranger lunch box belonging to the truck driver's son, abandon the truck driver without a word, get a job at a gas station, flirt with a guy planning to hike the Pacific Crest Trail, run away with him to the forest, ditch him while he disassembles the tent for the fifth time, lose yourself in the forest, have a staring contest with a bear, lose, play dead, come back to life, write a letter to Tulip, find an albatross with a broken wing at night, take the albatross to the ranger station, fall in love with the big, awkward bird, read your letters to Tulip while the bird recovers, volunteer to help nurture the forest, get into birding, release the albatross back into the wild, get offered a job that would pay more if you had a college degree, go back to school, write to Tulip, graduate, hear from your mother, your brother died, she misses you, wants to know when you are coming home, ignore all her attempts to connect, write to Tulip, study the flight patterns of albatrosses, make plans to visit Tulip, return to your bridge, ask strangers about the woman named Tulip, ignore your mother's shadow, ignore your mother on the park bench, ignore, ignore, ignore, find Tulip picking weeds outside an art museum, give her all the letters you've written to her, hold her close, promise to read them to her, ignore how skinny she's become, ignore her missing glass eye, ignore your mother's shadow, tell Tulip about the flight patterns of albatrosses, laugh when she double-dog dares you to imitate their call.

This Is a Story About a Fox

Bunny is a fox. She's just a different kind of fox. A special, one-of-a-kind, rare fox. Bunny stretches her fluffy fox tail and goes to the mirror to pin her ears.

"Good morning," Mother Rabbit says—a wicker basket with backpack straps tucked under her arm—coming into Bunny's room. She kisses Bunny's cheek and hops around collecting tufts of fur Bunny has shed in the night. "You're growing so fast."

"Yep," Bunny giggles, "into a big, strong fox!"

Mother Rabbit places a paw upon her chest. "A what?"

"A fox!" Bunny taps her foot. "Just look at my ears."

Mother Rabbit clicks her tongue, places her basket full of fur next to Bunny's bed. She hops to her daughter's side and gently unpins her ears.

"My bitty baby Bunny." Mother Rabbit flicks Bunny's tail. "You are a rabbit. Not a fox. A rabbit like your father and me."

"I'm a fox!" Bunny resists the urge to cross her arms; only bitty baby bunnies do that. "I'll prove it."

And she takes the pins from her mother's paws and goes down the hall to see her father.

Father Rabbit sits at the table drinking coffee, his carrot cigar held in the curl of his left ear for later. Bunny has pinned her ears into two perfect triangles and growls at her father—not in a mean way of course—but a good-morning-father kind of way.

"And hello to you, my little Bunny." Father Rabbit laughs then growls. "I like what you've done to your ears."

Bunny feels her chest swell. Of course father would understand. "I'm a fox!" Bunny shows her sharp teeth—also not in a mean way—while Mother Rabbit comes down the hall with her wicker basket.

"Of course you are." Father Rabbit nods.

Mother Rabbit clears her throat and—Bunny notices—her parents speak the language only adults understand. Filled with looks and head tilts and throat gurgles.

"Of course ... not," Father Rabbit stammers. "Because you are a rabbit."

Traitor.

"A rabbit," Mother Rabbit slips her basket filled with tufts of fur onto Bunny's back, "who will take this to Mother Sparrow."

"Why?"

"To keep her new chicks warm when they hatch." Mother Rabbit wiggles her nose into Bunny's neck.

"Since I am a fox," Bunny says between laughs, "I may eat Mother Sparrow."

"Don't tell her that," Father Rabbit says, biting into his carrot cigar.

Bunny puts her best fox paw forward and walks out the door.

"Good morning, little Bunny," Mr. Ram bleats while Bunny passes his fence.

"I am not a bunny." Bunny places her paws on the long wooden beam. "Look how sharp my claws are!"

"Claws?" Mr. Ram opens his one good eye real wide and leans closer for a better look. "Rabbits don't have claws."

"Exactly." Bunny smiles and continues on her way.

"Bunny!" Pony gallops up to Bunny and they nuzzle their noses together. "What happened to your ears?"

Bunny will have to explain the change in her appearance carefully to Pony since her friend gets excited over the smallest things.

"I–am–a fox."

"I thought you were a rabbit," Pony says, trotting two circles around Bunny.

"I used to be," Bunny extends her long tail, still fluffy but not a puff of cotton like in the storybooks Mother Rabbit used to read to her at bedtime. "But now, I'm a fox."

Pony sits in the middle of the road, repeating the conversation to herself. Bunny rolls her eyes, leaving her friend to her puzzling.

"Well," a fox lounges at the base of Mother Sparrow's tree, "what do we have here?"

"Hello," Bunny waves.

The fox rises, tail whipping in the air. The same way Father Rabbit's ears do when he hears trouble coming.

But Bunny isn't scared. "I'm a fox."

"You?" The fox covers his mouth with his paw. His body shakes and–from the back corner of his mouth– Bunny can see how sharp his teeth are.

"I am!" Bunny flashes her teeth, too. "See?"

"Oh, yes," the fox steps closer, "very sharp."

"And my claws!" Bunny flexes her paws, her little nails poke out.

"Very useful for catching prey."

Bunny gulps and, for the first time, hops back. She worked so hard to learn how to walk and this one hop will set back months of progress.

"I can scream, too," she whimpers and feels her embarrassment rise into her pinned ears.

The fox does not hide his laughter this time, causing the leaves in Mother Sparrow's tree to tremble.

But not Bunny.

Because foxes don't eat foxes.

"Let's hear it then." The fox growls, drool dripping from his chin.

Foxes don't eat foxes.

Bunny tilts her head back. She screams, her pitch a little too high for her liking, but she'll fix that with a little more practice.

"See?" She smiles.

But the fox doesn't answer. His claws dig into the dirt, tail steady, and ears bent back. Bunny knows this stance. She's practiced this stance in the mirror. Teeth rubbing together, eyes locked on their prey—on her. But, no, that can't be right because she's a fox.

She's—

The fox leaps and Bunny's ears come loose, wrapping around her eyes.

"Bunny!"

Pony?

The ground shakes and a loud yelp fills the air. Bunny unwraps her eyes and sees Mr. Ram headbutt the fox into the air. Pony runs to her side, Bunny's parents struggling to stay on her back.

Mother Rabbit scoops Bunny up in her paws and kisses her all over, which Bunny doesn't mind. Father

Rabbit checks the area before nuzzling Bunny, his ears warm like Bunny's favorite blanket.

"I saw the whole thing!" Mother Sparrow flies down from her nest landing in Bunny's basket. "She was so brave!"

"Like a fox!" Pony kicks and neighs.

"Like a fox." Mr. Ram lifts Bunny on his head.

She holds onto his horns, watches her mother nuzzle her father.

Yes, Bunny thinks*, like a fox. A special, rare, one-of-a-kind fox.*

Father Peach Tree

I am 12 years old when my father says goodbye. Not because he's leaving, because he's not. He cups my cheeks within his palms and promises it's nothing like that. Just that spring is coming faster than he—than any of us—expected. That it's time for him to shed the clothes he's wearing, to take root in the garden, and blossom into a peach tree.

My mother files for divorce, but because she can't divorce a tree, she decides to start over. Not like my father, whose feet spread throughout the garden soil, arms sprouting branches. My mother packs her suitcase and mine. *Take care of your brother,* she says, and I'm hurt she's not taking me with her. She'll return my suitcase with only a picture of her and her new husband inside. Signed *Wish you were here* on the back. On the day that she leaves, she accidentally steps on my foot while walking out the door. While waving goodbye to my brother who is suddenly there, who suddenly exists, who is suddenly wrapping his fingers around three of mine.

My father sprouts leaves when my brother tells me he hates me. Because I won't let him date until he's 18. Because he stole our father's car. Because I found a joint in the cupholder, an empty beer bottle wrapped in his shirt, a couple of pictures of naked girls while looking through his phone. *Why do you even care,* he says, before slamming my bedroom door.

I've moved into my parents' bedroom because my mother has a new life with her husband and 4-year-old twins and my father is a fucking tree that hasn't grown a single peach. *Why do you even care?* I can hear my brother slamming his fists into the wall. I try to remember why, when I never did before. When my father said goodbye, I don't remember my brother being there. When my mother took my suitcase instead of me, I don't remember him following the two of us to the door.

I try to do better. I try to spend time with him. I try to talk to my brother about girls, about life, about our father becoming a tree. He never answers unless I feed him. Unless I bribe him with cash or food. *Why do you care?* When I ask him about his interests. *Why do you care?* When I ask him about school. *Why do you care?* When I bring up our father, ask if we should give him a trim because his branches scrape against the side of the house when it storms.

I take my brother out for ice cream and he ditches me as soon as his friends arrive. I didn't know he called them. Didn't know he had found someone outside of me. I tell him to be home by 10, not knowing I wouldn't see him for ten years.

I return to my parents' house, sit at the base of my father. I ask him if he ever thought about staying. If he knew he had a son. I'm still bothered that I didn't, that nobody told me I had a brother until my father and then mother left. Until I was forced to take care of him, that brothers are very different from sons.

My father and I have different variations of this conversation. Somedays, I call my brother Sam or Davis because his real name escapes me during these talks. Mom is now Charlene who posts about her new kids graduating from high school. *I'm selling the house*, I say, because I think it's time I left, too. To live out of my car, to travel or live just off the highway. I check my father's branches for peaches but they remain bare. *You tried*, I say, to him more than me.

I try to call my brother, try to tell him something that I haven't before, but I have no idea how to reach him.

I pack the suitcase my mother sent me when she loved me. I call the Realtor on a flip phone I bought at Walmart. *I can't sell with that thing in the garden. Are you sure we can't cut him down?*

No, I say, which I probably don't mean since the peach tree serves no purpose.

Tell them about the peaches, I say, even though there are none.

There are none, she says, and I tell her to tell them anyway.

I meet my brother in Chicago when we are both old and so different from who we once were, we mistake strangers for each other. We eat hotdogs topped with relish in the back of my van. *Sometimes, I wanted to be invisible, he says.* I wipe my mouth with the back of my hand. *You were, until,* I abandon the rest. We both know what happened. Charlene's still using Facebook from her new home in Hawaii. My brother travels the world taking pictures of animals for magazines and museums. *And you?* he says, leaning in close like I'm about to tell him a secret. *What do you do?*

I return home to find a lawn full of peaches. I toss one to my brother whose taken a few days off from his job. Who worries, who takes pictures of me and my van and the peaches that cover our lawn. *I could never sell the damn thing,* and I bite into one of the peaches. The fur cradles my tongue. The juices taste sweet. The pit already gone.

The Five-Enders Club

We pose beneath the height requirement in front of a roller coaster named "Griffon," pretending we are too short to ride. Janice jokes that she might be too tall, shares the story of the teenage boy who was beheaded by a coaster.

Not this roller coaster, but a different one. A group of teenagers gathers around Janice, stands shoulder to shoulder with us, while she goes on about the boy's hair still tangled in the tracks. How, when you reach the peak, you can hear his initial scream.

The boys eat up Janice's story. They dare each other, place bets, see who can ride in the front row without fainting, without screaming, who can walk away from the ride without puking. The girls pick a boy to cling to, pretend to be afraid, though we know to place our bets on them.

We were girls once. Girls who clung to the arms of someone we believed to be stronger, braver, and in many ways better than us. Halley gathers our group together, whispers that we wait a while, teenagers being how they are.

We ditch Halley's plan when a class of middle-schoolers shows up. We'd rather be sandwiched between the two age groups than witness two teachers fumble in this heat because Becky wants to ride with Simon but Simon wants to sit in the back with Miranda who—no one has noticed—has sweated through her pants and is waiting for the opportunity to sneak out of line.

Dakota lingers a bit too long for our liking. The new girl in our group—The Five-Enders, ever since we lowered the age requirement. She's a new forty-fiver, our first, her shoulders already reddening from the sun. Her gray is non-existent which is why Janice was against her joining.

We voted and I, the sole sixty-fiver, won, which really burned Janice up until I shared my plans for Dakota's initiation. We are ex-wives, empty nesters, cancer and car accident survivors. Home wreckers and emotional wrecks. Book-clubbers and movie-goers and birders and gossips and, I tell Dakota, she could be all or one or some of these things, too.

If she can survive the Griffon.

A floorless, red dragon of a roller coaster that takes you 200 feet into the air, dangles you because what's a risk without second thoughts? We're waiting in line when Miriam makes Dakota swear to sit in the front row. Dakota suggests that someone should stay behind, hold the bags, take pictures, plan where the group goes to eat.

"Told you she wasn't one of us." Janice removes her wallet from the pocket of her blue tracksuit pants. Ever since her wife gave her an ultimatum—the details Janice refuses to share—she's dressed to run. Will even take off in the middle of a conversation.

I swat Janice's wallet away. "Give her a chance."

I hear Halley ask Miriam about the lump by her spine which is now a lump on her lung. "I feel pretty good, considering." Considering her kids either waste away in her basement or are out pretending to be in rehab until caught. Considering we've had to bail out Miriam several times financially, mentally, or vocally when her voice isn't strong enough alone.

They start to bicker when Janice interjects, claiming that she's done more in her seventy-five years of living than both Halley and Miriam's fifty-five. I find Dakota sneaking towards the edge of the line like so many who forget to remember the weak stomachs or fear of heights.

"You've been through worse." I know I have, with more miscarriages than I can count and thirty years of marriage spent with a man I love who wasn't sober for twenty-four of them.

"You don't know me." There's some bass in Dakota's voice which I can respect.

"I know you want to join us."

I hear Halley snicker, tell the other girls that we should make Dakota sit on the outside. I ask her how work's going over my shoulder which gets her to mind her mouth.

Halley's job is her five grandkids. Fifty-five and worrying about diapers, babysitters, and tuition all over again.

"What's your story, anyway?" We all have a reason for joining just like we're all a little afraid why a forty-fiver is tagging along to witness our tragedies.

"My twin sister," Dakota stares at the teenagers being herded into their lanes, the next ride coming is theirs. "She died on a coaster."

The entire line gets quiet. Even Janice kicks at the cement flooring, looking for a place to plant roots.

Dakota says the coaster was a wooden one, the operator of the Griffon saying, "Of course," before we all turn and hush him sounding like a pit of snakes. Dakota clears her throat. Says she begged her twin, Carolina, to go. Teased her when she hesitated, protested "when she offered to hold the bags."

Something happened on the tracks, a term Dakota can't remember, that caused the coaster to speed up instead of slow down. On their third go-around, her sister still didn't realize anything was wrong, screaming and laughing the entire time. "She kept saying, we're flying!" Until the brakes kicked in and their bar released them, Carolina taking off and Dakota left holding on.

"I blame myself."

We know that's true, the same way we know her parents blamed her too in the way parents do, pretending you take up enough space for two kids while reminding you that you're the one who survived.

The Griffon pulls up and the teenagers part, making our group the next in line. We look at each other; we look at Dakota, who nods and takes a step forward.

I catch her by her arm, "you don't have—"

"I can't remember," she turns and smiles that smile we all know—the smile we'd forgotten we had, "the last time I talked about Carolina." A smile that hurts so much but we've learned how to tolerate the pain.

Soba

Buckwheat flour veils the hands of the Black woman in the window. She draws the attention of crowds who leave fingerprints upon her reflection. Gaze as her hands form cylinder towers she destroys with her fists. Flattens and forms dough layers that remind them of the blankets they pile and stow in their closets. When her brown eyes rise from her creations, they wonder if she sees them or herself in glass. They wonder where she came from; some even feel the question crawl from their minds to the back of their throats. But her eyes drift back to her work, to her cutlery and boiling water shrouding her dark form in a steam cloak. Besides, who are they to disturb her.

And who are they to ruin the stories they tell with the trivialities of reality.

Yūrei
The children swarm around her window, a colony of murmurs dressed in uniform. At night, while their parents tuck them in, kiss their cheeks and

foreheads, the children tell them about the ghost that haunts the Soba shop they pass on their way to school. Their parents never believe them, such talk will induce nightmares, and the parents force their children to swallow these stories before turning off their lights. Instead, the children confide in each other. The sound of the woman's Soba kiri against her wooden cutting board reminds them of the woodpecker nibbling at the tree they dare each other to climb while their teacher's back is turned. Many of the children follow strands of steam that ascend from bursting bubbles, remember the scent of the cigarettes their teacher smokes, the ones that carry the scents of their parents.

Onryō

The teenagers avoid pressing their palms against her glass, believing the Soba woman laces a bit of herself within every noodle, so every customer walks away with a piece of her. After all, she is a creature of vengeance.

The girls are in love with the idea of heartbreak, envision the woman's rage captured in every bubble so that, when the water boils, you can hear her wrath like the long shrieks of a night wind that steals hats, newspapers, and unwanted scraps in its wisps. When it pours, the teenage girls tilt their heads back, open their mouths, and drink her tears.

The teenage boys think she is a woman of fire; her rage swells in the broth of her victims. Stirs in her customers' stomachs until their bodies burst into flame, beacons summoning her. Through pursed lips she devours their souls the same way they slurped the noodles she slices. She emerges from their homes covered in ash, and emits a warmth that reminds anyone who touches her window of the soups their mother's made when they were sick. This is how she summons her victims.

Why else would a woman, surrounded by heat and steam, not sweat unless she were made of fire?

Jibakurei

The tourists learn the existence of ghosts from their guide, some bound to the place where they died. They assume this is why the woman wears a mask. To hide her rotten teeth, silver poured into the pits of un-manicured bone, her punishment for eating the noodles she cooks. The tourists wonder the secrets she'd tell if only her lips could part. If the Soba woman is capable of a smile. They tell jokes, make faces, and perform plays, but still the woman refuses to smile. They decide her mask also hides the red thread that binds her lips together. Her cause of death: suffocation on the words she could no longer release. When the guide tells them her mask is to ensure the woman's breath does not touch the dough she rolls and molds and folds, the tourists take her picture and move on.

Ubume

The owner's wife smiles at the stories she hears from the entrance of the Sunaba. Her ghost, who smells of sesame oil and soy, drifts into the night after work hours, abandoning the owner's wife to deal with the memories that haunt her. The owner's wife leaves her husband to his counting, goes to their room, and closes the door. She watches her little ghost become a woman in the moonlight from her bedroom window, wonders where such beauty hides during the day. On the windowsill, the owner's wife keeps a rock. The name of the daughter she lost somewhere between a push she wasn't ready for and a breath her baby never took, written so many years ago by her husband in their daughter's blood. The owner's wife traces the letters that form her baby's name with each step her little ghost takes away from her. Feels the weight of stone in her palm increase in the years she sees reflected in the black Soba woman. Years her daughter will never reach, her eyes forever unopened.

Ikiryō

The rickshaw driver wipes sweat from his forehead, whistles the songs his grandfather taught him while his small body balanced on the back of a bicycle. He doesn't know a life without balance and wheels, hauling the weight of customers, back bent, a ghost who slips between cars. This is why he waits for her, though he's never prepared for her silence. He smiles, traces her face, steps closer until their foreheads touch. Anything to know she stands in front of him. The woman emits a heat that the rickshaw driver forces himself to withstand because of her eyes, wavering in the water she holds, swollen, and carrying every shade of brown in their irises. Sometimes, he is unsure if the same woman meets him at night. Sometimes, her hands are stained in the remnants of flour; sweat beads along her hairline but never falls. A woman who moves without sound but can be felt.

The rickshaw driver loves what this woman might be.

The rickshaw driver fears what this woman might become, should he approach her window and listen to the stories the people tell.

The Patron Saint of Keys

Tecla doesn't remember being born. Only that she is a girl painted black and white with no sound of her own. When the saints gather and offer their praises regarding one another's beauty and achievements, Tecla attempts to stretch her vocal cords among them. She licks the shapes of their names, their beauty, wants to share her thoughts on the saints and all of their achievements. However, she never makes a sound, the other saints passing her like a breeze.

Only the Patron Saint of Lost Things acknowledges Tecla's presence. They lead the child, hand sculpted from the fabric of the lost gloves of mortals pressing against Tecla's back, to the flower garden. In their palms, the Patron Saint of Lost Things summons marbles, socks, coins, and shoes, and Tecla adores them all. Not their shapes or colors, but the sounds they make. The heels of shoes when crashed together. The rigid edges of coins along her teeth. The static socks create when rubbed together, the thundering cries of marbles when warring over territory.

The Patron Saint of Lost Things plucks a peony from the garden. Within its petals, Tecla sees visions of the mortal realm. They say that Tecla will one day become a patron saint, responsible for guiding and protecting these mortals. Tecla tries to protest, to question, to sigh. What kind of patron saint could she possibly be if no one can hear her reply?

The peony unfurls revealing, perched on its petal, something Tecla has never seen. A mortal sits in front of a box, its upper lip propped up by a pole. The mortal runs her fingers along long buttons that look like the girl saint. Tecla tugs on the Patron Saint of Lost Things' robes, pointing to the source of the sound. They call this box a piano, the keys singing harmonies when pressed. Tecla presses on her chest, but doesn't make a sound, instead listens to the sounds of mortals.

She hears the click of a lock unlatching, the chorus of keys chiming together on the carabiner clipped to a janitor's belt. Tecla spends hours in the garden with all these sounds until the Patron Saint of Lost Things finds her. They alert Tecla to the dangers of the mortal realm, to never take what is not truly hers. They warn that, in doing so, Tecla may throw off the balance. After all, mortal have a tendency to worry.

However, Tecla cannot stop thinking about the keys, their sounds, their shapes, and sizes. Ignoring the warning from her friend, there's no way the mortals would miss one key, she ventures into their realm.

She decides to steal a single piano key and stores it in the pocket of her dress. But then she notices the door key and a key to a safe-deposit box. Next thing she knows, Tecla is five blocks down, promising to simply borrow the keys she collects. When her pockets are full and her small legs tired, she returns to the realm of the saints.

Once alone, she clinks her keys together but is disappointed by the sounds they make. A piano key does not sing when paired with a car key. The safe-deposit box key is overwhelmed by the janitor's keys. Even her rare garage door key denies Tecla its song.

The mortals stir in their houses and cars, alarmed that their keys are gone. They check their pockets and seats and shelves and each other, but none of their keys are there. They summon the Patron Saint of Lost Things, furious that their keys are gone.

They do not understand, nor do they know, where the mortals have left their keys. *How could the Patron Saint of Lost Things not know where lost things are?* The mortals, in their anger, tear apart the sock-locks of the Patron Saint of Lost Things. The mortals pull on their charger arms and legs, poke behind their button cheeks. Peel away their sunglass eyes, bellow words Tecla doesn't know.

Give us our keys! Give us our keys! The mortals chant, and Tecla cries out, it was me! That she stole the keys, that she's to blame, but the mortals cannot hear her. The other saints gather, shake their heads and pray for the foolish mortals and pray for what remains of their friend. For the Patron Saint of Lost Things who cries for their help, but the saints aren't permitted to interfere.

The girl saint, with the teeth of the stolen keys biting her damp palms, remember she's not like them. She's not a patron saint, not yet, and decides to follow her friend's advice. One by one, Tecla returns the keys, retracing all of her steps.

The final key, the piano key, she places and listens to its song. The mortals, all drawn to this singular note, follow its echoing call. In following the steps of the girl saint, they find their keys where they left them. In jars, under tables, as a mirror for their rat. In between couch cushions, in the palms of guilty teenagers, beneath beds that aren't always their own.

Tecla gathers the pieces of her friend, rebuilds them from the lost things of mortals. Once the Patron Saint has regained their mouth, they whisper how proud they are. A new sound washes over Tecla and, above, are the other saints. They whistle and applaud and shout Tecla's name, raining peony petals down upon her.

The Patron Saint of Lost Things shows Tecla a singular petal, the mortals all finding their keys. They start their cars, unlock their doors, play their pianos and sing together. They offer their thanks to this new patron saint, who guided them in retracing their steps.

Is This Really How It Happens?

You cheated

Then I cheated

I tried to cheat, lips puckered behind the bleachers with Levi Paterson, but then I thought, is this really how it happens?

I started thinking about you

I didn't want to

I couldn't help it

I started thinking about you and Hazel from chem

Unless you also kissed Hazel from band?

Did you?! How many "friends" do you have?!?!

I started thinking about you and whichever Hazel with your tongues in each other's mouths hoping your braces cut her

Her tongue

And I'm about to kiss Levi knowing you kissed Hazel in the janitor's closet while I waited for you to go to lunch thinking is this whole kissing thing really supposed to be so easy?

I didn't kiss Levi

I wish I did

I wish I wanted to

I thought I might have liked to, especially since he seemed interested in me

Not like how you used to be, always trying to hold my hand in secret under the table.

I can tell Levi thinks a lot about what he wants to say before he actually gains the courage to talk to anyone

He always notices when I'm wearing a new dress, and we both have a love for converse and Animaniacs

I thought those things might have made us kiss compatible

He shrugged when I changed my mind and left me because I guess I'm just that forgettable or leavable or whatever

Unlike you and the Hazels

Did she cut herself on your braces? I did, the first time we kissed and you were so worried. Afraid you ruined the whole thing.

Why weren't you afraid this time?

I'm afraid

Not of you

Definitely not of Hazel

To never be kissed again

To never have someone to worry about me again

I gave you my heart

And you cheated

And Levi just shrugged and walked away

And it's not fair that it's so easy for both of you

And for Hazel

Because I love you

And I want this to be hard for you, too

Abernathy_Resume.docx

Sybil Abernathy
Resume
Address Will Be Provided if
Offered Position—Philadelphia, PA
Ask Me to Drinks First
sybil.abernathy@gmail.com

STATEMENT OF INTENT
Highly skilled teacher looking for an adjunct position at a university because, somehow, I still only qualify for an entry-level job at the college level. Already overworked and underpaid but wish to apply my experience to educate undergraduate students and open their minds to the truths that academia continues to ignore.

EDUCATION
M.A., The College of Cathay Williams and Stagecoach Mary
Area of Focus: English and
African-American Literature   **May 2011**

B.A., Euphemia Haynes University
Area of Concentration: Early Childhood Education
Minor: Mathematics   **May 2002**

TEACHING EXPERIENCE
Mutineer Pioneer High School
High School History Teacher
September 2019 – Probably December 2020

- Required all students to read the Table of Contents of their U.S. History books in preparation for their first quiz. Questions included: How many times are Native Americans mentioned outside of Columbus, How many times are the lives of Africans explored before they are kidnapped from their homes and enslaved, and How many chapters are dedicated to any one woman who helped build the foundation of America? All students passed with a collective answer of zero, zero, zero.

- Encouraged students to research and portray any historical figure erased from U.S. history in order to educate their classmates. Dean Rickards borrowed his father's suit to teach the class about Hiram Rhodes Revels. Cheyenne Amos performed a monologue written in the voice of Jackie Mitchell, and B.T. led a word puzzle exercise based on Sequoyah's Cherokee Syllabary.

- Before this section's presentations, we "dropped" the U.S. History textbooks in a trash compactor. We watched the seams split, the hard covers break, my letter of eventual termination clear as the brief glimpses of history left on the shredded pages the students scattered like confetti

Westview of the Riverfork Middle School
Middle School Math Teacher
September 2015 - June 2019

- Resisted the urge to panic when Madison Shepherd found herself on the wrong side of our classroom door during lockdown. Practiced various breathing techniques while keeping an even tone, telling Madison that she was very brave, to keep her palm against mine through the glass, and that the lockdown would be over soon though—at the time—I wasn't sure.

- Stayed after school with Mikaela Tillons to tutor her in fractions. *My mama can't help,* she says, *cause she has to work. Grandma's too sick and Daddy just spits. Says 'You don't need them no way.'*

- Noticed that some of the students would linger in the halls or at their desks during lunch. *I can't buy lunch,* they'd say. Went to the principal, who claimed there was "no room in the budget" and that "it's their parents' responsibility." Brought the issue to the cafeteria workers and started the GIMME program where locals could donate lunches for hungry students to eat during lunch time. The rrincipal took charge of the program—even has local restaurants cooking meals for the kids monthly—after I was fired for "insubordination."

Edgewater Valley Elementary
Second-Grade Teacher
September 2011 - June 2015

- Confiscated Fidget Spinners used as Frisbees, notes passed between Natalie Ramos and Grayson Phillips—I never opened them—and Cindy

Chestnut's pigtail after Marcus Nevins managed to cut it off with scissors that I did not give him.

- Comforted Cindy Chestnut while she cried about how her new haircut made her look like a boy—which it did. Red nosed with puffed, freckled cheeks brought the Howdy Doody doll lurking in my grandparents' attic to mind, causing me to hug her just a little tighter.

- Injected EpiPen into the fatty part of Grayson Phillips's thigh after he went into anaphylactic shock during lunch. After the paramedics left with Grayson asking for his grandpa from the back of an ambulance, I checked his lunch box and found a half-eaten chocolate-marshmallow brownie. Natalie Ramos latched on to two of my fingers. My mommy wanted to make sure, she said, she asked about marshmallows in her note. She even made some without just in case. I cried in my empty classroom after the final bus left that day.

Sunnyday Sundae Preschool
Kindergarten Teacher
September 2004 - June 2009

- Quelled the Great Glue War on the eve of nap time, January 2006. Explained to both parties—The Gentlemen of Elmer's and the Ladies of Avery Glue Stick—that both were wrong to assume one glue was better than the other. That eating or slurping—depending on preference—would lead to a mad teacher, very mad parents, and very upset tummies.

- Potty-trained Miley Harris, though questioned who was training who. When I asked why don't you sit down to pee, her response was my body, my rules.

- Often found myself sitting beside Timothy Wilkins while we waited for his mother to come pick him up after school. One day he asked if I could listen. If he could tell me a secret. He told me that his mother is like Winnie-the-Pooh, always wanting honey but her honey looks like baby powder. He tells me he's like Piglet, always helping her and scared and small but does his best to wipe the honey away when she makes a mess. I'm like Piglet, he says, always waiting, hoping she's not bothering the bees for more.

SKILLS

- Survived (and Passed) the Praxis Exam
- Intermediate Levels of Patience
- Curriculum Development Beyond Dead White Guys
- Captivating Storyteller When the Voices Permit Me to Speak
- Ability to Teach Three Classes in a Row on Five Hours of Sleep, Two Cups of Coffee, and Pixie Stix (Preferably Red)
- Capable of Avoiding Alcohol but Definitely Smokes Weed, Sometimes with My Students but Mostly with Their Parents
- Unwillingly Frugal, Surviving on a Diet of Ramen, One Shower per Month, No TV Time, and Plenty of (Unwanted) Cardio
- Ability to Locate the Best Stairwells, Closets, Basements, Bathrooms, and Forgotten Classrooms for Optimal Periods of Crying, Outbursts of Anger, or Moments of Sheer Depression When Feeling Underappreciated, Overworked, and Overwhelmed.

Comical

He's a comedian. She's his lover. He pushes past her, into her hotel room, before she can invite him in. She remains in the doorway. He sits on the bed. *Close the door*, he says. Not in the voice she likes, when he's just delivered the punch line, listening to the audience laugh while he takes a long drag from his cigarette. Not like in the moments after the laughter dies and he says five, ten, seven, four words on a good night to get the audience going again. No, he says close the door in a whisper, paranoid, checking a watch that's never been on his wrist. Like someone's followed him. Listening to him, not a paying audience but reporters. And she closes the door because reporters mean tabloids mean gossip means his wife finds out about her and about him and about both of them which means he can longer see her and when she hears the click of the door as it closes she wonders if he really sees her as anything outside of this room. That, maybe, he wants to. So, she offers him a drink, determined to ask him later. Not tonight later but, eventually, later. He's nervous, doesn't know what to do with his hands, so he buries them under his legs. *Wine, if you have it.* She doesn't. Of course she doesn't, and the fact that she doesn't lingers in the room. In the stain he traces on the floor before he kicks off his shoes. In the scabs she picks around her fingers until they bleed as she goes to him. She's nervous. There's something about him. About the way he holds her when they kiss. How he tries to suffocate himself between her breasts. What happened to her clothes? What happened to his? *What happened?* She says, running her stil-bleeding fingers through his hair, grease collecting under her nails. Blood trails marking his scalp. The scent of cigarettes caught in the dust particles that leave him. *I got the laugh,* he says, kissing her nipples, body tensing, hands becoming sure as they rock with her on him on a bed with springs that wheeze. *I got the laugh*. He's crying. She kisses his nose, his stubble, his neck, wonders if he's ever this emotional with his wife. He flips her so he's on top. She stares at him, at his face, the face his wife must miss. He might love her. Might be in love with her, if he might be in love with anyone. *What happened*, though she knows because she was there in the dark, watching him smoke and tell jokes about his drunk mother and his father's gambling habit and her, as his wife. *My wife*, he says into her neck, over and over again, leaving a kiss with every W formed. She clings to him, forces him to be fully, completely inside of her. *I can't love her like you*. She knows. She wonders what love looks like between him and his wife. She kisses his ear. He says something into her shoulder. She knows. He finishes. She's still holding on but doesn't know to what or why. He kisses her. *Love?* His tongue leaves a trail as it traces down her body, between her breasts, her stomach, between her thighs. She holds on. When this is over, he'll go home to his wife, the woman left out of his jokes. She'll ask him what happened. He'll blame alcohol, cigarettes, the lack of love from his parents, but never her. Never the her that is his wife or the her that is she in this hotel room on this bed with his tongue beckoning her to come and as she gets closer and closer she forgets about his wife and love and who is where because she is here coming and when she is finished he takes his time kissing her limp legs until they twitch and he makes her come again until she is finally finished and he is finished getting dressed and she thinks about asking him to stay. But his wife exists, again. Is out there, waiting for him, again. He kisses her, not like before, not how she likes. He kisses her like he kisses the air between himself and the audience before saying his name. Before saying goodnight. Before they applaud and beg him for more and he tells them they've been great and he ... leaves them. Like he leaves her. Like, she knows, he leaves everyone who might want to love him.

At the Only Friendly's Open When the World Ends

The fries arrive soggy but crimped. The smell of grease lingers in the red leather seats that suction to exposed skin. The waitresses wear red shirts with exaggerated triangle collars. Say *Welcome to Friendly's* with signature smiles, cover the big *F for Friendly's* on the back wall with their final paychecks, play hopscotch on brown tiled floors. Balance black trays on their shoulders, carrying the Mushroom Cheese-Mania Burger, the Sriracha Burger, a serving of Buffalo Mac & Cheese.

At the only Friendly's open when the world ends, no one talks about the fires. How the sky is always red, how their lungs burn and everything tastes like lead dipped in Tabasco. Nobody talks about how the children can't stop coughing. How the women blister. How the men are gone. How someone—or everyone— thinks there's still time to try again to save the world or—maybe—time to save themselves.

At the only Friendly's open when the world ends a woman reenacts her first date with a crash-test dummy, pretending he is the man she should have married. She orders the Clown Sundae. He orders one Monster Sundae with extra horns made of Reese's Peanut Butter Cups split in two. Their waitress smiles that signature smile, asks *will that be all?* The woman nods, offers to pay the waitress in cash, *says could you hurry? We've got somewhere to be.* The waitress nods but leaves the money so the woman takes it instead. She folds one bill into a paper crane, the other into a heart.

At the only Friendly's open when the world ends, a woman kisses a dummy, pretending he is the man she should have married while reenacting her first date. She tastes peanut butter and vanilla on his tongue, sits back and whispers, *Delicious.*

The Joke

Thiago invites me over and I hesitate to go.

I ask my mom if I can go over to Thiago's like it's no big deal, like he hasn't ignored me for the past two months.

She says it's good that we're talking again.

We're not.

Because boys can't be friends with girls.

Girls have cooties and laugh too loud and twitter and chirp like crows—which cackle, not twitter and chirp—and smell like fruit.

Which is, apparently, a gross way to smell.

The door to Thiago's apartment is unlocked, the 0 that used to form Apartment 1802 lying flat on his family's welcome mat.

His door tells me a joke, one eight two, and I think about telling Thiago.

Candles are lit on the kitchen table, the Virgin Marys gathered for a monthly prayer, book club, or gossip session while someone prepares their drinks.

A wad of blue gum clings to the hallway ceiling.

A baseball card pokes out from Thiago's bedroom door.

I don't recognize the player.

"Hello?"

"In here."

Thiago sounds like he did when we were in the haunted house, him clinging to the back of my shirt and asking if the scary part is over yet.

I lied and said it was.

I told the truth and said it was.

He never opened his eyes.

He is crouched on the closed toilet seat in the apartment's pink bathroom.

His mother's choice.

"What are you doing?"

"There's a rat."

"Where?"

Thiago taps on the closed lid.

"What do you want me to do about it?"

"Get rid of it."

I think about telling him the joke.

"I can't with you sitting there."

One ate two.

"Fine," he hesitates when trying to move around me.

He does the same thing at school, dance around me like he's forgotten the steps while I'm suffering from stage fright.

Then his boys come bail him out and I'm the one left looking stupid.

"You didn't pee or anything did—"

"No!"

That gets him moving, hops right on the counter.

"Only a little."

His butt almost slides into the sink's mouth and I laugh for what feels like the first time in a long time in front of him.

"Shut up."

He punches my arm.

He laughs.

I know boys aren't supposed to hit girls.

But the contact feels nice.

I lift the lid.

Thiago was telling the truth.

A giant rat floats in slightly yellowed water.

Only a little my ass.

"What if he's alive?"

"I think your pee finished him off."

Thiago doesn't laugh.

Just looks at me the same way he did when I promised the haunted house wouldn't be *that* scary.

It was.

But it wasn't with Thiago.

"Give me something to poke it with."

"Like what?"

"You got a plunger?"

"I don't know."

"A magazine?"

"No."

"Your toothbrush then."

Thiago thinks really hard about this, and I want to say I'm kidding, but not really.

"I got an idea."

Thiago leaves.

I think about picking up the dead rat with my bare hands.

Thiago would have to tell his boys that story.

Or he'd tell his boys he picked up the rat.

Leave me out of it.

Forget my name.

No, he wouldn't do that.

Then he'd have to admit he'd peed on the rat first.

Thiago comes back with a clipboard.

"Where'd you get that?"

"Don't worry about it."

His voice sounds small and quiet like whenever his dad calls from "upstate."

I take the clipboard and poke the rat.

He doesn't move.

He's dead.

"Some lady's been coming by."

He rests his chin on my shoulder.

Like he used to.

When he didn't want me to see him cry.

"She asks if I'm happy here, who watches me when Mami's at work, what time Mami gets home from work, if I'm safe, am I eating, how many meals a day, how much."

I know the answers to some of those questions aren't what adults want to hear.

Answers that shouldn't be written down.

"You can't tell anyone you were here."

"I won't."

"I'm serious."

"Me, too."

It feels good to have secrets again.

I manage to lift the rat onto the clipboard.

"Open the window."

"Why?"

"You want me to throw him in the trash?"

The weight of Thiago disappears but not before I hear him click his tongue in my ear.

I hate that sound.

He knows I hate that sound.

The window fights Thiago, but he eventually pries it open.

The same time the rat pries his eyes open.

I scream and Thiago nearly falls and the rat is shaking all the extra water and pee loose from its fur.

All over my face.

Some of the drops land in my open mouth.

I think about screaming.

I'm about to scream.

Thiago covers my mouth.

The rat touches his hand.

He screams.

I throw the rat and he hits the closed part of the window.

Thiago clings to me, shouts, "do something!"

"Get it!"

"Raylee!"

He starts breaking things up with Spanish—words he never shared with me—but I'm caught on the fact that he still knows my name.

"Ray!"

The rat.

He's on the floor, confused and looking at Thiago and I like we have all the answers.

I do.

For once, I do.

I pick him up.

With my bare hands.

And throw him out the window.

Thiago slams it shut.

Like there's a chance of him coming back.

Breathing hard.

Like it was all him.

We're alone and Thiago is panicking, his breathing not slowing down.

I think about the joke.

"Do you want to hear a joke?"

My words suck the air right out of him.

"You should go."

They say boys shouldn't hit girls.

"Thanks, I guess."

I wonder whoever said that realized words can slap, too.

"Promise you won't tell?"

Can get you right in the gut.

"Promise?"

Where it hurts so bad.

"Ray?"

You think your heart might stop from the shock.

The King of Tent City

I'm in love with the King of Tent City, Chicago. Me, the woman sipping on gasoline. I'm on a pilgrimage to find the last Texaco in the U.S. when I see her, The King of Tent City, in an oversized army jacket and newspaper crown. This is our home, she says to her followers who peep from behind tent-flap doors. *We have a right to be here!* Then, she looks at me, points her gloved finger at me. *We all have a right to be here.*

I am the woman sipping gasoline, sometimes from an old Campbells soup can. However, I prefer straight from the nozzle, diesel, with a hint of Strawberry starburst. The King of Tent City notices me, notices how I can maneuver my way around these stations. How I mingle with truck drivers, sneak shots from minivans, trade cigarettes, lottery tickets, and road maps marked with the best pit stops per state in exchange for gasoline sips. The King of Tent City says she likes how I work, says I could be of use to her.

I prefer to drink gasoline straight from the nozzle, diesel, with a hint of strawberry Starburst. However, because The King of Tent City asks, I get my shots straight from the tank with a crazy straw shaped like a Shell sign. While the citizens of Tent City stop traffic with their cardboard signs asking for money, for help, for the kindness of strangers, I sneak up to the traveler's gas tanks. I drain their supply, force them to stop and refuel at the nearest gas station. The King of Tent City waits for them at 7-eleven, discusses the mistreatment of her subjects. Hands out pamphlets made from pizza boxes, newspaper letters, even mini-tent figures made of soft drink cups and condiment packets. *Support the cause,* she says. *Save Tent City,* we say.

Because the King of Tent City asks, I get my shots straight from the tank with a crazy straw shaped like a Shell sign. Though, if I'm honest, I still have Texaco on my mind. I find comfort in the license plates of strangers, gain the courage to ask if they've been to Texaco. *We haven't been there in years!* The drivers share stories of their parents, of road trips and stalled cars. The King doesn't mind these conversations, encourages me to continue. Memories shared tends to lead to more money and more money supports the cause. I sometimes ask about other tent cities, ask if they are thriving, if they welcome newcomers and kings.

Though, if I'm honest, I still have Texaco on my mind. *I have a map,* I say, while kissing the King, and show her my planned route. *You could stay,* she whispers into my hair. *You could leave,* I hold the map higher. Maybe she isn't seeing it as clearly as I do, and I tell her all that she's missing. On the road, there are not battles to be fought. There's adventure, new sights, and I tell her all the people she might meet if she'd just come with me. Are you bored here? Never, I say and pull her closer to me. *Then you expect me to abandon my people?* I bite her skin to hide my anger because yes, I really do. I bite my King harder, watch my marks pock her skin like Google Maps pins. She clings to me so I have no choice but to collapse and remain inside her tent.

I have a map, I say, while the police pat me down, my head pressed against the hood of a patrol car. We are trespassers. A disturbance. We are unruly disruptions, a band of vigilantes who dance around burning barrels. My Tent City King fights until the end, leads her army of refugees with weapons made of broken glass bottles. Of used needles, tent poles, and broken street signs for shields. She charges towards me, towards the Chicago P.D., and I can't help but smile. My bite marks swell in the sun, a map marking landmarks I've traveled on her. The war doesn't end in a massacre, though she'll say it will. We are held captive for three days. *A new Tent City,* I'll ask while she stands beneath the underpass where her kingdom once stood. *No,* she'll sigh, then kiss me, and then she'll ask how long do I think it will take for us to find Texaco?

Your Husband Wants to Be a Cardboard Cutout at the Last Blockbuster on Earth

Just think, he says, *me, a part of history*. And you do. You think about your husband as an inanimate man. You wonder if that's how he feels about you, about your marriage. If this dream—that's what you choose to call it—was inspired by something left unfulfilled by you. Imagine, you hear him say to no one at all, and you do. You imagine that you are no one.

When your husband tells you he wants to be a cardboard cutout at the last Blockbuster on Earth, you dye your hair the color of lilacs. You shave your legs, your armpits and arms. You shave everywhere, except your head and eyebrows. You drape your body around the house because that's what desirable women do. You drape your body across the couch, on countertops, on the bed you still share with your husband. You even drape your body over the banister. You call him darling. Tell him you love him. You stop him from leaving by draping yourself in the doorway and tell him, *I want you*. He kisses you, wraps his arms around your waist. *Wait for me,* he says, and you think while watching him go that this phase is finally over. You think that you've won, until your husband returns hauling deconstructed cardboard boxes. *To study,* he says, and you retreat to the bathroom. You lock the door. Turn on the water. Watch it fall from the showerhead. You drape your naked body along the base of your empty tub. Curl in on yourself and wait for your bare body to prune.

Your husband practices being a cardboard cutout around the house. He poses in the closet, stilled hands offering you your favorite coat. In the kitchen, he holds a root beer float pretending to call someone to claim it. You reach for the root beer float, but he holds it out of your reach. You watch the condensation run down his arm, notice how chill bumps rise. The calls come a month later. The principal of the local elementary school finds your husband in the middle of the street posing as a crossing guard. A student studying forensics finds your husband posing in one of the chalk body outlines of their mock crime scene. A Realtor complains your husband is scaring potential buyers. A curator for The Liberty Bell says, *Tourists love posing and taking pictures with your husband as George Washington* and wants to know how much he charges per hour.

You confront your husband when you find a cardboard model of the last Blockbuster on Earth beneath the bed you and your husband used to share. He stands at the end of your driveway, clothes absorbing his sweat, the knees of his pants covered in grass stains. He holds a sign that reads, *A Nice Lawn is Appreciated by Everyone!* You hold his face in your hands, *This has to stop*, you say, but he doesn't respond. You pinch him. Run his foot over with the wheel of your empty trash can. Bump him with the back of your car. But your husband refuses to move. You cry because the neighbors are watching and the neighbors are watching because you are screaming move! In the end, when your voice reminds you of the sound of cardboard tearing apart, you lean in close to your husband with puckered lips and hiss, *You blinked.*

After you ruin your husband's dream of becoming a cardboard cutout at the last Blockbuster on Earth, you find him on the couch, staring at lifeless ceiling fan blades. His odor hits you on the third day. After a week, you wonder if you did the right thing. One night, you place his head on your lap and browse through the new arrivals on Netflix. You pause on a documentary about the rise and fall of Blockbuster. Your husband squirms, his toes curl and release. You gently pull each strand of his budding beard, whisper *OK*, and press play.

You met your husband at your local Blockbuster, which isn't the last Blockbuster on Earth. The guy who would become your husband was once the VHS rewind guy. The guy who—when you asked for a light family movie—recommended *The Brave Little Toaster*. You feel like Kirby, the vacuum, at the edge of the waterfall when your husband no longer walks but waddles. When his movements grow stiff, a cardboard triangle sprouting from his spine to prop him up. You tell your husband this at the end of the documentary. He kisses your knee, your neck, your lips. *Can we shower?* he asks, and you nod because he needs to. Because, you think, this is something you can do together.

Your husband wants to be a cardboard cutout at the last Blockbuster on Earth. He poses in movie theater lobbies dressed as Darth Vader, Godzilla, and Willy Wonka. *I need to practice being human,* he says the night you ask him *Why Willy Wonka?* He leaves you earlier each day, returning later and later without apology. You always kiss him when he comes home and try not to notice when he starts to waddle again. When the cardboard triangle stretches up his spine, when his cheek starts to taste like shipping boxes and duct tape. You stop shaving but keep dying your hair, this time a mixture of green and blue. *Your favorite colors*, he says, and for the first time the compliment just sits between you.

You notice your husband is leaving you when you discover fewer of his clothes occupy your closet, replaced by your new outfits, scarves, and shoes. His mugs, toothbrush, comb, and all his costumes vanish, and you know there's no point in trying to find them. One day, you wake up on your husband's side of the bed. That's when you realize, he's gone. You plunge your face deep into his pillow. You inhale, ready for his scent, and choke on the smell of you.

In This Story, You Are the Magician's Rabbit

1.   In this story, you are dying from the toxins found in the white paint you soak in before and after every show. The Magician claims your brown fur is too common, too reminiscent of the mud pit he rescued you from. White catches the light. Dazzles and provides a starker contrast while you dangle above his black velvet top hat. Children beg to pet you. *Gently*, the Magician instructs. You feel their fingers strum your rib cage. Seek nourishment in their whispered *I love yous.*

2.   In this story you aren't a rabbit—not a real one— but you'd like to become one. The Magician's mother reads, *The Velveteen Rabbit,* and you learn that love is the way to become real. You snuggle close to the Magician, especially during thunderstorms, and hope this is enough. You love him, despite the numerous times the Magician locks you away in his backpack during school, attempts to launch you into space—you land on the roof—and forgets to find your lost button eye on the playground even though he promised. You wonder if you are loving right when he loses you under the bed. Forgets to take you to college. Calls you thing

when his newest assistant finds you covered in dust. *That old thing*, he says, and you think your feelings— you're still unsure if you have them—are hurt. You must have feelings because what you are experiencing is happiness when the Magician performs again. Removes a dime from your ear, removes the tablecloth without shattering a plate, even makes you disappear into the attic. He'll make you reappear, that's part of the trick, and you'll wait and wonder if this version of love is enough.

3.   In this story, you witness the Magician make ten doves appear from beneath his cape. The sound of their beating wings reminds you of the ticking of your husband's pocket watch. The Magician will witness the tip of your tail as it disappears into your burrow. You sprint past a mirror that turns your reflection upside down, books with blank pages, and slip through the center of a hall shaped like an hourglass. You find your husband seated with the Mad Hatter, the March Hare, and the Dormouse, tea splattered everywhere. *A very merry un-birthday!* they say and offer you a teacup made of carrot cake.

4.   In this story, you pull a magician from your hat. Take a bow amongst a horde of rabbits thumping the ground with their feet.

5.   In this story, the Magician—having lost his prowess for magic—releases you back into the wild. You don't turn around, not even when you hear him say, *I'll miss you.*

6.   In this story, you read an article about a woman who cuts off her hair to avoid her husband's grasp.

Since you don't have hair, you tie your ears into knots. When The Magician reaches into his hat, all he finds is air.

7. In this story, you pull yourself out of a hat.

8. In this story, you eat all five of your children. Because you are starving. Because of your instincts. Because your husband is watching from a different cage. Because you are in love with one of the Magician's doves. Because you are in love with the Magician. Because you hate the Magician. Because you hate that you want to be loved by the Magician. Because you don't want your babies to have this life. Because you never wanted this life because you are always hungry because you are always caged because they are always watching and waiting and always yearning for more.

9. In this story, you are happy. The Magician is famous, which means you are famous. You have a residency at the Mirage Casino and Resort. You sleep with Montecore, ask him what it was like to bite into Roy. You take an apprentice who says *I love you* by accident, but then on purpose. The Magician and your apprentice create new tricks, perform them while you watch from box seats. In your will—you know you'll only live to be ten, maybe twelve—you ask not to be taxidermied. *Make me disappear*, you write, *deep into the soil of Mr. McGregor's garden.*

10. In this story, you are the final act. That's what the Magician says, *You will be my final act.* The curtains part to reveal you onstage, beneath a spotlight spraying specks that remind you of snow. You can't see the audience, but you can smell them, all peppermints

and gum, chicken parmesan, except that one guy who ordered the salmon. The Magician whistles from offstage and you turn to find him smiling. He feigns applause and you understand that this, this moment, is meant for you.

Can I Take Your Order?

Order extra fries drizzled with chocolate. You shouldn't have to say "melted chocolate" because you say "drizzled" so it's clearly implied. Ten ketchup packets, just in case. You never know what might happen on the drive home. A burger would be nice. Treat yourself. Three patties, tomatoes, no pickles, light mustard, ketchup, all wrapped in lettuce.

You are, after all, watching your figure.

Not really, but tell the teenager on the other end of the voice box this. Say, *I'm watching my figure.* Don't let the sound of static embarrass you.

Instead, talk about your mother. The measuring tape she wrapped around your waist before every ballet class. How she compared you to other little girls sinking deep into their pliés.

Your ass gon' be trouble, she'd say, while the other little girls covered their ears.

Don't let the sound of static embarrass you.

Remember your father with a rib bone hanging from his mouth. Your uncles drooling grease, smacking on ox tails, chitlins, pig feet, chicken wings, feet, breasts, thighs, and gizzards. You tried that once, not the gizzards, but parading around with a bone in your mouth. *Somethin' wrong with that girl,* your uncles said.

Your daddy wouldn't face you.

That's when you ate the gizzards. Held them in your hand above your grandma's favorite cooking pot in a closet all your own.

Ask how much for a slice of apple pie. Laugh when the teenager in the voice box says, *They nasty*, after you miss hearing the cost.

Talk about pie. Apple, pecan, sweet potato, that one cherry pie you threw up when you were 16. Leave the memory there. Or don't. If you want, talk about how the women in your family take any bit of you they consider swollen and pinch and pull while sucking their teeth.

When you were a baby, it was cute.

Five, and they start to worry. *What they feeding you, girl?* They say while struggling to raise you over their heads.

You are a big-legged girl at 12. *Just as big as you wanna be.*

Sixteen and you're *grown assed'ed*, just like your mama said.

Baby having a baby, she said.

Except, you decided not to.

Again, you don't have to talk about that.

The teenager in the voice box will ask if you want extra napkins. Ask if you want a cupholder for a drink you don't remember ordering. He'll tell you to pull around to the second window.

I thought I paid at the first? You say.

Listen to the sound of static.

Change your mind. You ordered a burger and deserve a bun. Clutch a twenty in your palm. Practice saying, *actually, I'd like a bun please.*

Practice saying, *Keep the change.*

Stare at your reflection in the sliding window. Your swollen cheeks. Arms beneath a sweatshirt that once belonged to a college linemen version of your father. How your stomach plumes over a belt strapped too tight. You can't see it, but you know it's happening.

The teenager behind the voice box appears, smiles, and offers you a brown bag with a greasy bottom.

Your order, he says, and you hear him. You swear you hear him.

And you ask, *How much do I owe?*

In Terms of Beauty

Death finds me in a Kohl's fitting room and I ask if I'm to die with thighs that no longer fit into a petite pant and face wrinkled and plagued with spots, my back to the fitting room mirror, which reveals a thong pinched between my ass reflected back at me instead of the beige underwear that cradles me and the spanks that grasp the thighs that are now without stretch marks. I ask Death how long do I have and Death caresses my face, kneads my skin tight and whispers *My darling, you never made it out of surgery.*

Vagabond Mannequin

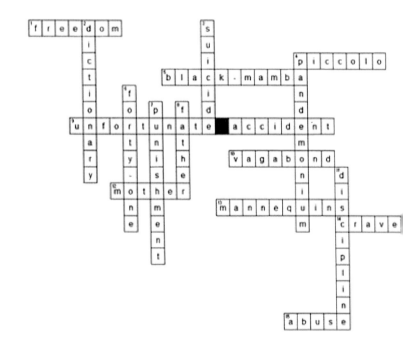

Across

1. You are alone in a room of many. You are without the father who loved you once. You slip into cramped spaces until you find yourself outside. You pose as a stranger's daughter. A child playing with a friend. Someone's older sister. The roles you play lead you back to the train tracks, back to your father. You climb on the steel rails with a promise that you'll jump off as soon as the train comes. There are so many words that appear in your tears, and you think of all the places you'll go, the forms you'll take. You wonder is this feeling the definition of:

4. The nickname your father whispers when he calls to you at night. Hint: He gives you this nickname because of the sounds that escape your flared nostrils while he plays the role of your guardian, keeping vigil

Down

2. There is only one book in your home, with a red gloss cover, the pages filled with columns of words printed in black. A book you surrender yourself to until your mother discovers you'd rather be reading than listening to her contradictory critiques of the daughter she never wanted. What is the name of the book your mother steals from you, whose pages curl before red flames puncture its center in a fireplace you never knew could generate such heat?

3. What's the one word you will never say because you know if you release it into the world, you will have to face the reality that your father was not the man you wanted or needed him to be, that he abandoned by your bedside while you sleep.

5. This type of snake is known to be one of the world's deadliest. It has a coffin-shaped head and is faster than most people can run. Hint: You whisper the name of this snake when your mother's shadow extends under the frame of your bedroom door.

you knowing the life you would live without him?

4. Think of a word you would use to describe your life. Hint: Think of all the times your mother held your body suspended upside down in the air, your world once in color now a shade of red and silence before going out. The long hours your father spends with his Glock 19 in his lap. You shouldn't know so much about guns at ten years old, so you imagine his gun is the family cat you call Butters.

9. The reporters swarm around you, wanting answers about the man whose torso is somewhere between the tracks and wheels. Whose head no one can find. What's the phrase that mixes with their spit to dismiss this whole occurrence while you bite your tongue until it bleeds?

6. How old is your father the night he takes you to the train tracks? The night you could hear the train in the distance but your father continued to back away from you with a smile that disappears in a mixture of smoke and light, your screams swallowed by the shrieks of metal?

10. The fights between your parents were at first verbal battlegrounds. Now, your house is a war zone and you are forced to dodge chairs and your favorite rag doll with curls made of yarn tied with ribbons that are stained with drool. If you manage to escape, you climb to the roof of your house, become a statue poised to perfection, and wait for someone to notice you. You decide that you would like to be a person who wanders to new places without obligation. You want to be a:

7. When your mother forces you to stand in the corner of the living room with your back turned to her, your feet stacked inside the mouth of a bucket filled with ice, this is a form of:

12. The title of the person who pretends you don't exist, until you do. Who chases you through tight hallways, your footsteps a symphony that rises and falls. Who steals patches of your hair for safe keeping. The blood she summons when cracks form beneath your surface.

8. The title of the person who smells of discarded peanut shells you find tucked between the floorboards of your home. Who lets you ride on his shoulders when your eyes are different shades of purple, swollen, and tender.

13. You see the beautiful women made of fiberglass in the windows of department stores—women who make your father scratch the stubble of his beard. You know his itches surface when he's nervous, nails scraping the pinprick hairs you nuzzle into when your mother finally drinks herself to sleep. You beg him to take you inside, and he does, and you hold his hand the entire time while you guide him to the beautiful women who refuse to acknowledge your presence. Your father squeezes your hand and tells you in a voice he uses to soothe your boo-boos and bedtime stories that these women are:

14. Describe yourself in this moment. Hint: This used to be your favorite word because you heard it pass between your father's lips to describe you once, until you looked up the definition.

11. Your mother tells you to go outside and pick a stick. When you return, you pull down your pants because you know this is what you're supposed to do without question. You feel the sting of tree bark as it knits into the welts that form. This is the definition of:

15. You are surrounded by women who smile and offer you paper cones filled with water. Their eyes stare at your broken arm, how your left eye swells and weeps. They tell you your mother is with the police. That they are sorry about your father. They give a name to all the things your mother has done and that name is:

How Fortunate
We Are to Be Cursed

Mrs. Blaythidd believes someone has cursed her. She believes this because her stomach reminds her of a wet pancake, and she has stretch marks and age spots and wrinkles. Her teeth, which she is sure were in her mouth last night, are in a glass on her bedside table. Once she changes and figures out how to regain her teeth, she goes downstairs and finds three grown men at her table and a cat, perhaps her cat, lounging under one of the men's chairs.

"Morning, Mom!" they all say with Cheerios in their mouths.

That can't be right, she thinks, because her sons are 4, 7, and 11. Certainly not men and, certainly not, *these* men. Perhaps they are the ones who cursed her.

"Did you curse me?" she asks the strange men at her table.

The three men glance at each other, then at her, and Mrs. Blaythidd decides that, no, these men couldn't have possibly cursed her. Curses are complex things and these three can't keep Cheerios and milk in their mouths.

Three women walk into the room with a flock of children following each of them. Like a flock of geese, Mrs. Blaythidd thinks, the children not cute enough to be ducklings.

"Mom thinks she's cursed," says one of the men, and the women all take turns laughing.

Perhaps one, or all three of the women, can read Mrs. Blaythidd's thoughts and that is why they cursed her.

One of the children, the last of the flock, is crying with snot running from his nose. He's a mess, and everyone can see he's a mess, yet the men and women do nothing. The child breaks from line and walks over to Mrs. Blaythidd, arms stretched, and screaming.

But Mrs. Blaythidd has no time to worry about the crying child because some of these children have stolen her eyes. Some have stolen her nose, their mistake, and one little girl has stolen her husband's stubby fingers.

"Where is my husband?" She asks one of the men.

"On the porch," says one of the women.

She finds her husband on the porch and notices that he, too, has been cursed.

"Someone's cursed us," she tells her husband, taking a seat beside him.

"Probably the cat," and she hears her husband laugh.

The leaky child, who is no longer leaking, comes out and has the nerve to climb onto Mrs. Blaythidd's lap.

She doesn't know why, perhaps she's sick, but she kisses the leaky child's finger. The leaky child smiles, so she smiles, and she rocks this child while sitting next to her husband and she listens to the terrible noise in the house until it's not so terrible and all Mrs.

Blaythidd can think is, perhaps, they might all realize how lucky they are if someone cursed them, too.

These Worn Bodies

Dry leaves save the fire suckling on branches stained with pine sap from dying. Matdiey takes an ax to one of Mistress Whitaker's good chairs and feeds the pieces to the flame, careful the fire doesn't choke. She used to love the smell of burning pine and maple until her daddy was sent down the road to chop lumber for a neighbor who claimed the wood was too wet to burn.

Behind closed eyes, Matdiey only sees the body of her daddy swinging from barren branches, toes tipping over dried, curling leaves.

She keeps a bit of her daddy and mama in the pocket of her apron tied around the layers of clothes she wears to keep the winter chill from finding her skin. Strips of cloth from her parents' clothes wrap around rocks the Whitakers won't miss. Matdiey rubs her thumb over the tattered remains of her daddy, joining Mistress Whitaker outside on the porch for—what she keeps in her mind—the last time.

The Big House could burn behind her and Mistress Whitaker's eyes would never leave the black iron gate wrapping around Good'Night plantation. She insists the house remain warm for when "they" return, the word dying a little more in Mistress Whitaker's throat with each passing day. The women keep watch over the men in gray uniforms beyond the gate, wrinkled and hunched, covered in bloodied bandages with tongues too caught up in what they've seen to speak. Matdiey has never seen so many men missing so much of themselves. However, none of these worn bodies belongs to Master Whitaker, the two Whitaker boys, or Matdiey's husband, Solomon, even the ones dangling from wooden carts.

Still, Mistress Whitaker has Matdiey search them all.

Slaves used to drift in the opposite direction in the early days, careful to avoid the soldiers. Some carried tattered clothes. Others clung to silver spoons, pocket watches, or other objects dead men won't miss but might help the living when scrounging for food later on. Mistress Whitaker spits on the porch planks—their white paint peeling—every time something glistens in the hands of a slave.

Though those objects do look good in the hands of freemen.

Matdiey thinks on her own stash wrapped in one of the Whitaker boy's sheets tucked in the roots of a tree just beyond the gate. Every morning, before Mistress Whitaker stirs, she walks to her stash to make sure it's there, touches the bits of silverware polished by her mama, empty picture frames, pins, and other things the soldiers deemed too useless to take during one of their raids. She moves these stolen pieces a little farther every day. With every sunrise, Matdiey takes another step farther from Good'Night until her heart stills enough for her body to keep going.

"Have Hadley start dinner," and Matdiey's thoughts return to Mistress Whitaker, a small woman who whistles when she talks because a gap in her teeth she used to shield with a fan no matter the season, until a soldier ripped it away from her.

"Hadley's gone, Miss."

"Then get Sarah."

"Also gone," the tip of Matdiey's tongue is pricking the roof of her mouth by the time she realizes the tone she's let slip. Hazel eyes that turn gold when the light hits them right stare up at her with such force, Matdiey takes a step back and lowers her head.

"You watch how you speak to me, girl."

"Yes, mistress," Matdiey caresses her mama's bit of cloth in her apron pocket.

"Set them right."

Most times, Mistress Whitaker's words sound like the end of a thought, though Matdiey remembers the woman's been known to carry on conversations with the air or her reflection.

"I should—" Matdiey swallows the rest. Hadley ran off with the first Black man she saw walking, Sarah not too far behind with a baby on her hip. Matdiey thought about joining them but didn't want to leave the rocks of her parents behind. After she grabbed them, Hadley and Sarah were nowhere to be found, and even in a crowd, Matdiey couldn't bring herself to step off Whitaker land without papers.

"Solomon."

There's a smile itching at Mistress Whitaker's lips as she rises from her seat. She's spent so many days sitting, Matdiey forgets they stand eye-to-eye with each other.

The two women spend some time in the quiet, Matdiey grasping her parents. Mistress Whitaker biting and curling her lips.

"He'll be on." Matdiey wants to believe these words as they echo in her bones. She bites back the other words she wants to say, how Mistress Whitaker never said her husband's name until now. Instead, Matdiey allows the force of her anger to move her down the steps. The rocks of her Mama and Daddy curl next to one another, playfully patting against Matdiey's leg.

"Get back here."

Good'Night plantation swallowed up more lives than Matdiey knows, discarded more people than she can hold in her heart—including her mama—caged and carried off without time for a goodbye.

"Matdiey."

She has one hand on the black iron gate. The other gripped by Mistress Whitaker. Matdiey looks back at the panting woman, brown hair with strands of gray clinging to her red face cracked with wrinkles borrowed by a woman beyond her years. Hazel eyes, now brown like Matdiey's, trembling with veins creeping in. They remind Matdiey of the lashes swelling on her back. She can feel their bones collide every time Mistress Whitaker tugs at her fingers. She thinks on how Solomon kissed the hand Mistress Whitaker holds, whispering about freedom in the dark before sneaking away to find a blue uniform.

Matdiey likes the idea of her Solomon waiting for her somewhere in blue.

She tears her hand away. Listens to the iron gate wail as it swings open. Matdiey steps through, grabs her bundle, and gazes at how her feet fill the footsteps of all who've made it this far

A Girl Called Boy

We call her boy when she shoots spit from the side of her mouth drowning an entire ant colony. We call her boy when she's up to bat. Boy on strike one. Boy, strike two. *C'mon, show me something,* the pitcher says, mitt jerking air between his legs, and we shout *Boy, please* and hold on to our braids because boy when she cracks that bat against that ball's ass it zeros in on that pitcher boy. We call her boy when we ask her to sleep over. Boy when our mamas say *Who?* We tell them she's a girl and they ask if we're sure and honestly, some of us aren't. We watch her use the girl's bathroom, sing in the girl's choir, become our comrade when it's girls versus boys in gym. We call her boy when we invite her to sleep over. Boy while we do our nails, our lips, our hair. *You ready, boy?* We take turns gripping somebody's daddy's razor. Electric boy. Smoothed edges, boy. As close as you can, boy. *This is your dare, boy,* and we take turns carving shooting stars into her head. We trace them with our fingernails as proof of our fine work. We call her boy when we pull her between us, legs crossed, lips glossed in popcorn butter and pepperoni pizza grease. Ask her if she's ever kissed a boy? This girl we call boy gets real shy. Gets real quiet so we promise to teach her how. We open a bag of Twizzlers, bite one end and offer her the other. *Kiss us, boy*, and we each wait our turn as she bites and bites and bites. We call her boy when she deepens her voice. Boy when she binds her breasts. Boy when she keeps her head shaved close, wears clothes that sag, disappears into the boy's bathroom. Boy when she petitions to play football. Boy when she wears a suit to prom. We call her boy when she asks each of us to dance. Grasps our hands, tells us all the ways we're beautiful while we inhale her cologne. Hazel-eyed beauty. Intelligent, sweetheart, funny-as-hell beauty. You smell like an apple pie, vanilla, crawdads, and Old Bay beauty. *Boy you crazy,* we say, but we laugh and forget about those other boys. Boys who grab us, who tear us, who hurt us for fun. Those old boys and young boys. Boys we knew. Boys we don't. Boys who heard us say no and boys we thought we loved. Boys who watch us take a turn with her, fists curled, sweat soiling their collars. We call her boy when we confront our teachers, *It's not like her to skip school.* We call her boy when we text her phone, call her house, throw rocks and sticks and books at her window. Boy when we see her next time on the news. Boy curled up in a trash bag. We call each other, ask *How did this happen? Ask Why didn't we look for our boy?* Some of us confront her mother who says she lost her daughter years ago. *Boy*, we say when the door slams in our face. *Boy*, as we prepare his funeral. *Boy*, when we stand up and tell our stories. *Boy*, who many of us will remember as our first boy, our only boy, perhaps the best boy we'll ever know.

The Origin Story
of the Forgotten Girls
Left Behind by Their
Absent Mothers

Before our mother runs away, she makes us pancakes that remind us of ducks. While our father straightens his tie, we create ponds out of syrup and reeds out of toast. Our ducks quack and flap their pancake wings and one even mimics Donald Duck. We are sad when our ducks transform into crumbs, but our mother promises us that, someday, they'll return.

After our mother runs away, we can't stand the waddling and quacking and even the feathers of ducks. The youngest of us researches duck suicides during mating season and our father stops wearing a tie. The oldest of us hides in hunting tree stands and waits with her slingshot drawn. Every time a duck flies over her head, she aims but never shoots. *I never shoot,* she always says into what used to be our mother's pillow.

Before our mother runs away, she tells us how pretty we are. How lucky she is to have two beautiful girls with beautiful toes and beautiful eyes. We smile at our mother because, in this moment, she is ours. We see ourselves in the hair she keeps pinned beneath her scarf, in every tooth that peeks through her lips.

After, when we are certain our mother has run away, the oldest of us only smiles at strangers she meets on street corners and bars. She asks them how much they are willing to pay, because our father has sold all his ties. Because our father has stopped going to work and, sometimes, he doesn't come home at all. *How much?* The oldest leans through opened windows, puckers her lips, and winks. Because the youngest of us is doing well in school and deserves a chance to get out. *You can make it,* the oldest of us tells the youngest when she comes home before the sun rises. The youngest of us always waits for the oldest, always sitting in the chair at the kitchen table, the one that faces the door. Even after the oldest of us leaves the money she's earned on the table, even after the sun starts to rise, the youngest of us sits and waits and waits until it's around the time Mother would have started making breakfast.

Before our mother runs away, she only has a single pair of running shoes, never worn, collecting dust by the door beside father's umbrella.

After, we go through her closet and find five, eight, fifteen pairs of running shoes, all stacked beneath her side of the bed.

Before our mother runs away, she used to tell us stories. Sometimes about dragons, about princesses, and talking animals. Our mother would make all the sounds, give voice to every character, and the oldest of us would beg for her to read the entire story again.

After our mother runs away, our father tells us stories. How our mother was the love of his life, how she was everything good in him. The oldest of us rolls her eyes, wearing a skirt that is too short and a shirt that is too tight, and claims she's too old for these lies. The youngest of us asks to be excused because she has an anatomy test tomorrow and the oldest of us thinks that she'll check under the youngest's bed to ensure there are no running shoes hiding there.

Before our mother runs away, she asks to play hide and seek. She counts to ten while the oldest of us hides in the tooshed out back. She counts to twenty while the youngest of us curls up with the pots and pans in one of the lower cabinets. She counts to thirty, until she doesn't count any higher, until the kitchen door is left open, and we remain in hiding. Only when we hear Father come home do we emerge. Only when he asks, *Where is your mother?* do we realize she never planned to find us.

After our mother runs away, our father dies in his sleep. We bury him with his favorite tie, hands clasped around an old pair of our mother's running shoes.

After, the youngest of us becomes a mortician. She counts to ten with a cadaver on the table. To twenty, and eventually makes it to thirty before forgetting what comes next.

The oldest of us no longer appears on street corners because, after, the youngest of us pays for the oldest to go back to school.

And, after, the oldest of us writes about the lives of the forgotten girls left behind by their absent mothers. An interviewer asks, *shouldn't it be assumed that the absent mother left someone or something behind?*

Not really, the oldest of us will say, *because the physical is separate from the mental.* The audience will agree, and the interviewer will too before asking, *But where have all the mothers gone?*

And the oldest of us will shrug, will straighten what once was our father's tie and say, *Perhaps they are feeding the ducks.*

Tuesday

I always find Tuesday, mask and gloves already on, lingering around the registers at 7 a.m. His name's not actually Tuesday—just like my name isn't Zombie—but when the world shuts down and you become one of the few who don't quit under the guise that you love people or your job or whatever thrown-together excuse matched with a plastered smile you deliver to your boss, you start to experiment with what you can get away with.

I meet Tuesday at register 2, the aisle with a cooler that stocks Red Bull. Where an array of individually wrapped condoms form a secret kaleidoscope behind the expired gum.

"Morning." He places his two Red Bulls, two condoms, and a box of black gloves, size small, on the belt. I swipe one Red Bull and pretend the smile I offer him isn't real. "Won't you get in trouble?"

I take the box of gloves, put a pair on, and place the box in my drawer. "Won't you?"

He winks and leans over the belt, pretends to browse through the gum when, really, he's checking how many condoms we have left.

I don't tell him I make sure there are always enough before I leave, just like I don't admit that he might be the only reason I'm still here.

I don't remember meeting Tuesday, only that his name tag said "Tuesday" on a Wednesday while he restocked the coolers with Pepsi.

"I have a thing about strangers, Sara."

"Do I look like a Sara?"

He laughed, which felt good since I just picked up this nametag from the back, the sound a welcome distraction from his overly greased hair.

"No." He reached for the last package of pink Starburst and placed them on the belt "You look like a Wednesday."

Somehow, that was enough. He made some joke about Humpday and I went on a rant about *The Addams Family*.

"Find me later?" he said after grabbing his two Red Bulls.

"Where?"

"In the back, breaking down boxes."

He walked away before I could tell him he forgot his Starburst. He never asked about them so I never told him I ate them all.

Tuesday pulls a black mask out of his pocket.

"There's nobody here."

He clutches the shirt fabric over his heart. I roll my eyes and put the mask on. Satisfied, he grabs one of his Red Bulls and offers me the other. I place it in the drawer next to the gloves.

"Find me later?" A condom dances between his fingers.

I always do.

During my break, I eat a bag of chips to get me through the rest of the day, then bring Tuesday his second Red Bull. In the back, the sound of him breaking boxes echoes throughout the empty hall and I hate to think that this is the sound of the apocalypse. He's standing in the trailer of an 18-wheeler and, when he turns and sees me standing there, he wipes sweat that isn't there with the back of his hand.

"Who ordered the Red Bull?"

He walks up to me, so close his nose touches my forehead. We are both without our masks, without our gloves, and I can feel his warm breath against my skin while he closes the door to the trailer.

In the dark, I can hear him swallow and search until my fingers touch his Adam's apple. He crushes the can, tosses it somewhere I can't see. Kisses me, traces my lips with his tongue. I lower my hands, remove his belt, find masks and gloves in his back pockets.

When we are naked except for our newly masked faces and gloves, we take our time trying to break each other. He knows I like when he nuzzles my breasts. He likes when I grab his ass when he least expects it. The way his gloves feel along my neck, me pulling his body closer to mine. Me on my tiptoes to press our masks together where our lips might meet, him turning me around, trying to resist.

But I can feel him leave a trail on my skin, which makes me shiver, which breaks him. His body too close to mine. The moan a whispered surrender.

And I'm thankful because this means I don't have to put the condom on. That I don't have to scramble in the dark and can just take his gloved hand in mine and lead him away from the door until I'm ready to stop. Until I'm ready to accept him and feel him and the sweat that dampens our masks. Until the heat of us makes me feel like I'm suffocating and—somehow—he senses this and presses his mask against mine.

And he takes a moment to touch me. To feel me with his gloves on and, every time, I break.

"Do you ever worry—"

I'm putting on my shirt and pants with my gloves still on when Tuesday asks. Worry about what this time? What today? The cysts in my breasts that I don't tell him about? The baby we both kind of want but maybe not with each other? Other things in our lives? Nothing about our lives or maybe something about what's happening around us?

When Tuesday doesn't finish, I try to start again.

"When do you think this will end?"

"Do you want it to?"

He thinks I'm talking about him and maybe I am. What are we after this?

I remove the gloves like they taught us, peel them so they turn inside out. I lost my mask, like I usually do.

Tuesday offers me another.

"I'm leaving," he says and, for some reason, I wait for him to ask me to go with him.

When he doesn't, I say, "I work another 7 a.m. on Friday."

His eyes widen and he stares at me too long.

I don't know what he was expecting me to say. I only know what I can't.

12 Moments
in the Life of a Fly

1. The maggot emerges from her egg nestled in a rotting banana peel and witnesses her 120 siblings stripping and eating pieces of their home. One of her 113 brothers nudges her to the edge of the blackened peel. The maggot learns the meaning of taste, of hunger, and how to feast like her siblings do. *Mother will be so proud*, she thinks.

2. The maggot learns to talk when she is two days old, much like her 120 siblings. While her siblings discuss moving on—their banana peel almost gone— the maggot demands that her nudge brother pick a name. *So I always know it's you,* she says, to which her brother—predictably—nudges her away. *How will mother tell us apart?*she asks, inching back to her brother's side. He doesn't answer. He rarely does, but the maggot likes that he doesn't talk about leaving, either. *Someone should be here*, the maggot thinks, *to greet mother when she comes home.*

3. Something unsettles the maggot, telling her it's time to cocoon. She doesn't understand this feeling

because she doesn't know what it means to "cocoon." Her siblings are restless as well, rolling around in tiny circles. The maggot's brother nudges her out of his way before inching off on his own. *Where are you going?* But— of course—he doesn't answer. *Mother will worry*, she thinks, watching her nudge brother slip away. Watching her siblings tumble. *No one should be left alone*, she says, and inches after her nudge brother.

4.   The maggot and her brother live in a green trashcan where they dine on feces and popcorn kernels. *When are we going back?* the maggot asks her nudge brother when they are four days old. *We're not,* he says, inching towards the far edge of the trash can and, because the maggot is a creature prone to habit, she follows him. When she finds her brother, a thick layer of brown sprouts from his base. *It's time,* he says. The maggot curls up beside him because her body tells her this is the right thing to do. *Byzantium*, she hears her brother say and, when she tries to respond, she finds that her brother is sleeping within a brown casing she assumes one might call a cocoon.

5.   The maggot is no longer a maggot when she emerges from her cocoon, but a housefly named Byzantium. She stretches her new appendages and immediately knows what to call them: legs, thorax, wings. *Brother*, Byzantium squeals, all six of her legs trembling, *brother come see*! But her brother is gone, leaving only bits of his broken cocoon and skin.

6.   After learning that her siblings are gone and her mother is probably gone, too, Byzantium decides to travel. She meets other flies, asks about their parents and siblings. *I don't remember,* they say, *do you?* And she

doesn't, except for her brother. *His name is Nudge*, she tells them. She wonders what he's doing now.

7. Byzantium is ten days old, much too old for wandering the skies and seeking solace in the arms of daddy longlegs. She settles on the wooden beam of a barn, perfect except for one neighbor who—when she only wanted to say hello—tells her to *buzz off* and flicks her with his tail back to her newfound home. *Serves you right*, someone laughs, *landing on a horse like that!* Another fly, this one with red eyes, saunters forward wearing a crooked smile. *Byzantium*, she says. *Zimmy*, he says, and shakes all four of her extended hands.

8. Zimmy doesn't remember his parents or siblings. Byzantium curls up beside him and tells him about her brother, Nudge. *I used to do the same to him*, she says. *I hope you don't see me as a brother*, Zimmy stammers. And she doesn't. Although she loved Nudge very much, she knows her love for Zimmy is different. *Are we moving too fast?* And Byzantium answers Zimmy's question with a kiss. *We aren't moving fast enough,* she says.

9. Byzantium lays her third batch of eggs in a half-eaten Happy Meal tossed into a dumpster not too far from home. That's 110, Zimmy cheers, hovering over their children. *Can we stay?* she asks even though she knows the answer. They've tried to stay before. Every time, Byzantium wakes on their wooden beam overlooking their rude neighbor called horse. She screams and demands Zimmy take her back. *I don't remember the way*, he says, and every time she realizes she doesn't, either. Now, with her third batch, she wonders if this is what her mother felt like, trying to stay, always knowing she couldn't.

10.   *Looks like I'm going to miss them*, Zimmy says, two hands resting on Byzantium's swollen stomach. His eyes no longer glow bright red when he was twelve days old and laughing at her foolishness. Now, they are worn with his fifteen days of living. *Stay*, Byzantium pleads. She listens to Zimmy's jagged breaths as he caresses her cheek. *Byzantium*, he says, and then he's gone.

11.   Byzantium delivers her fourth brood in the barn, her eggs nestled deep within horse's feces. *Take care of them*, she whispers, and leaves. The barn isn't home, not without Zimmy. She finds a discarded matchbox tucked away in a field. That night, Byzantium imagines the stars are her children, her siblings, her mother. One even hovers above her, red and steady, and the sight of it makes her weep. *I miss you,* she whispers to the stars.

12.   Byzantium is twenty-eight days old. Something stirs inside her, but she doesn't mind this feeling. Something brushes against her head, the gentlest touch she's ever felt. *Zimmy?* The touch presses harder. *Nudge*, she smiles, and tries to lift her head. Though her eyesight is failing, Byznatium swears she sees someone move beside her, the faintest warmth nestling against her. *No one should be alone*, she says, gathering what little strength remains to stay just a little longer.

At the Risk
of Missing My Heart

A troll watches me play during recess but nobody sees her except me. Nobody sees her except me, but I tell my daddy one night before bed. I tell my daddy one night before bed about a troll with a face like mine. With a face like mine, the troll presses her face against the chain-link fence and, sometimes, she calls out my name. She calls out my name, not like how Daddy does after he kisses my forehead goodnight, goes downstairs, and says my name into the phone over and over again. Over and over again, I watch my daddy pace from the top of the stairs muttering words I don't understand. Muttering words I don't understand, my daddy stops talking, stops moving, and I hear the troll speak. I hear the troll speak about loving and missing me, that I am her heart, that she deserves another chance. She deserves another chance, though I don't know at what, but Daddy seems to understand. Daddy seems to understand because he tells the troll she's had several chances and has failed every time. She has failed every time, that I understand, because I have failed sometimes, too. I have failed sometimes, and I wonder as I return to my bed, if this means that one day I'll turn into a troll. I'll turn into a troll, I whisper to my teddy bear, as Daddy comes to check on me. When Daddy comes to check on me, I tell him I'm afraid. I'm afraid of trolls, of failures, and the risk of missing my heart. The risk of missing my heart makes me cry in my daddy's arms. In my daddy's arms, with his big hands on my head and back, I feel safe from anything that might hurt me. I feel safe from anything that might hurt me, including from the troll that somehow knows my name. From the troll, who somehow knows my name, whose heart I've accidentally stolen and don't know how to return.

Draft No. 1

Perched on the indentation of her opening scene's first paragraph, The Woman watches as The Author of her story brings the rim of his 3 a.m. bourbon to his lips. At least, she likes to think her story fills the pages of his navy blue Moleskine journal, written in the black ink of the fountain pen his father gave him, the only acknowledgement The Author received for his dream of being a writer.

She wonders what it's like to dream. Perhaps that's what The Author is doing, standing alone in his living room, staring out the window. He doesn't write her dreams if he ever imagines them—his audience would rather know what is happening to her in the reality of his creation rather than a world that will never exist outside of her.

But what is happening in her reality?

Robert, who last week was Daniel, is just a name on the corner of a dog-ear page, red lines severing him. The Woman is thankful it was sudden, that she didn't hear his cries of pain as The Author cut him. She wonders why she remembers him. Perhaps it's because his name sits in the corner of the page of her first scene. Or maybe The Author left one small trace of Robert on purpose, not ready to throw away one of his characters so easily.

Or maybe The Author enjoys striking their lives with the tip of a red pen.

Maybe that was Robert's purpose.

She fears the same might happen to her, especially since The Author took the time to name Robert twice while she remains The Woman, a figure The Author sketches in between sentences.

She tells herself she is more than a definite article used to mark her gender. That The Author is in the process of creating her story, just taking time to mourn the loss of Robert. He was never a successful character. His only identifying trait was that he was her husband's best friend. The Woman glances overhead at the sentences swallowing Robert, her sentences, forming paragraphs and pages and still she remains nameless.

Her husband even has a name, a physical description, dialogue. His name is Adam, always has been. He dreams of becoming a detective. Not like the ones he watches on television but the ones he reads about in his noir novels he hoards in cardboard boxes. The Woman thinks her husband dreams with the noir filter on, flirting with femme fatales, shadows of the blinds leaving white and blank imprints on his face. The narrator of his story.

But he manages an independent bookstore, allowing her to hide between bookshelves to discover recipes and tricks to maintaining a stable home.

Why hasn't The Author given her a job? At least, outside of what her name, or most obvious quality, suggests. She is more than capable of handling one. The Woman is creative enough to create snowmen made of marshmallows, Hershey Kiss children with graham cracker sleds playing on a mountain of white cake and frosting. She is mentally aware of her presence on the page with the ability to move freely within the bound pages of The Author's journal. She exists, and doesn't her existence mean she has a purpose? Desires? What is her motivation? How does she contribute to the plot?

The Woman skips ahead a few pages. Learns that she is shy, her mind constantly working to solve crosswords and riddles once the house smells of Snuggle's Blue Sparkle dryer sheets and Lysol. Tells jokes her husband pretends to understand. She loves puzzles, especially when they are timed, and eventually shares this love with Adam. Two chapters later and they are working on a book together, her creating puzzles that his detective persona must solve.

And Adam takes credit for all her ideas.

The Author writes a scene describing the time The Woman gave Adam a wool trench coat and matching fedora, which he refused to take off even when it rained. When summer comes, Adam hides under the cover of trees, keeps the air-conditioning on high in their home and bookstore, causing the skin under her nails to turn purple. She uses the money Adam gives her, The Author deciding she is incapable of handling money, to buy him another trench coat, one that is water proof, and wonders if this is what love looks like to The Author.

Adam stops talking to her halfway through the draft, which she doesn't mind. The Author hasn't written her dialogue in yet, just quotes surrounding single spaces of air.

The Woman wanders through the rest, skimming stakeout scenes of Adam crouching behind dumpsters, pretending to be a customer in a diner, hiding behind a newspaper.

Adam interrogating someone in their basement.

Why didn't she notice this before?

She reaches the final page of the first draft. Adam is gone, not like Robert, but his presence is missing from the page. The Woman is alone, staring at her reflection in the kitchen window, rim of her 3 a.m. glass of wine leaving her lips.

She can do better.

She can handle a world outside her kitchen.

A drink that's not served in a glass whose neck you have to choke.

She can put on a fedora and trench coat and get into fights.

Narrate her own story while it rains, blinds leaving white and black imprints on her face.

The Woman wonders if Robert had these thoughts.

The Author returns to his seat, empty glass sweating remnants of leftover ice cubes. He picks up his pen, the red one, sharp tip cutting away at her scenes. Through her reflection in the window, her love of puzzles, her creativity, and everything she is. She runs, climbing over the sentences that make up her husband, seizing what remains of her life, her thoughts and feelings, wondering if they were ever hers.

Dragon's Keep

Tomorrow, the girl knight dressed in bronze armor, will stand before the dragon's lair with plans to avenge her knight mother. She carries the scarlet scale from her mother's final kill within her palm, her mother's sword at her side.

But tonight, the dragon nips her babies' tails while they play amongst splintered eggshells. Her dragon's flame dazzles the hues of red in her dragonlings' scales and she thinks *If only their father could see.*

A Letter to My Breasts

Dear Teagan and Margo,

Tomorrow, I'll show you to a stranger. Not on purpose, of course, but we know the changing rooms at the gynecologist's office are never private. We'll wear a Pepto Bismol gown and Margo will stiffen because of the draft caused by observational rooms, their doors left open just a crack to see the glow of ultrasound screens. Because of the one white vent blowing out dust particles, sounds competing with the murmuring of nurses while they flip through charts contained in manila folders with rainbow-lettered stickers.

Teagan, I know you will remember our college days, sleeping on the front lawn of the Kappa house wearing bedsheet togas smelling of piss-colored beer from glass bottles. Waking up next to Jim, Robbie, Henry and Robbie, Kyle, Robbie, or Mortimer. We loved to watch their chests rise in their sleep, never telling them about the ants that made these boys their Everests. We only asked ourselves *who names their kid Mortimer* and *we should have told Robbie ... something.*

At that time, only Margo knew what the two of us felt for him. I'm sorry Margo and, maybe after our appointment tomorrow–

Tomorrow, at our appointment, the stranger will lick her thumb and turn the page of a magazine she pretends to read. I know how to pretend to read because I pretended to read the essays our son wrote about his heroes, why the sky is blue, and his compare/contrast essay about bumblebees and Stalin.

Do you two remember teaching our son how to tie his shoes? He came home from kindergarten, Velcro straps in his hands. Our clever son figured out a way to cut them from his shoes with safety scissors because the children at school teased him for not having laces. He cried into Teagan while you, Margo, grew jealous, so I pulled him away from us and smiled. I told him I would teach him how to tie a perfect bow, to tie a tie and a bow tie if needed, which made him laugh while snot dried on his upper lip.

I didn't mention that we were terrible at tying knots. The four of us put the rabbit through the hole but he kept escaping. We'd tie his ears tight, but somehow, the rabbit wouldn't stay. Yet, we didn't mind, because our son was in my lap, head leaning against Margo until he fell asleep between the two of you. We held him as long as we could because we knew we didn't have many more moments left where the four of us could just be, where our son would just nuzzle against us.

I wish we knew then that he would teach himself how to tie his shoes, how he would learn to call us out on our shortcomings, call us gross, squirm from our arms, or toss a love you too over his shoulder.

Tomorrow, I'll compare the two of you to the stranger's breasts. I'll see them through the loose sleeve of her gown but I already know they'll sleep above her stomach without the shadow line of a wire bra. Not a spot or vein or hair in sight and, I'm sorry, but I'll be jealous. When our son was born, Margo, you were so happy you volunteered to feed him first.

Then he clamped and sucked—which is far worse than suckling—and you bled every time he cried.

Teagan, we all know you were selfish during this time, producing milk for a pump and not for the half-hour wails of a baby who needed you.

Not for the blood stains Margo left in my lactation bras or for me when I pleaded and massaged and held our son's lips to you. Maybe you refused to lower your standards to the hungers of a child when—for years—you've satisfied men. You, the larger of the two, the first these men reached for on the surface of trampolines, in mirror houses, and from the neighboring seat on an airplane while Margo and I slept.

I don't know about Margo, we know she's sensitive about being smaller than you, but I'm sorry I asked *are you sure* when you broke out into chills despite the sweat building beneath you. When the flight attendant stopped by our aisle, her eyes flitting towards the man pretending to be asleep next to us then, while holding the three of us in her gaze asked *Can I help you?*

I'm sorry I spoke up for the three of us and said *I'm fine.*

Maybe tomorrow I'll ask the stranger sitting next to me if I can help her, though, I'll probably just show her pictures of our grandbaby. She'll compliment our grandchild, say *Look at that smile,* and maybe I'll believe her.

And that's when she'll see the two of you.

You'll both lean against my Pepto gown, tugging my failure of a rabbit bow loose. The gown will fall and Teagan, you'll flex, while Margo attempts to retreat.

The stranger will stare at our veins. How our skin sighs around our weight. I'll consider reaching for my gown—but I won't. I won't because then this stranger will see the two of you kiss my stomach, my knees, the trace of my C-section scar.

Or maybe I'll think about Robbie. How he held you and kissed you equally. Of our son nuzzling between the two of you, giggling because he tied his shoes and ours. I'll think about telling this stranger why the three of us are here, nothing serious like cancer, just more fiberoptic cysts that need to be pinched and biopsied.

And maybe I'll ask this stranger why she's here, and, maybe, she'll slip off her gown and whisper something serious, like cancer, and we'll sit together pretending that we're comfortable in this cold waiting room while nurses flip through their manila-bound charts and the screens of ultrasounds light up dark rooms.

Yours, always.

Sausage People

Sunshine through the blinds mimics hall lights peeking through Girl's cracked bedroom door. The scent of cigarettes. The pop of Big Red chewing gum. Footsteps that make her floorboards cry.

A soft caress from the hand of her father's best friend while he lowers himself in the crook of her bent knees hidden under her covers.

His fingernails scratch her like sweet ant legs, tipping past the elastic of her pajama pants. *Don't it feel good girl?*

She swallows all the tears, chokes on every noise, making her body tremble under her covers. He takes Girl on long walks when her daddy is sober, through the woods and spits Big Red in spots he later tells her he'd bury her body. Wads like the one he leaves behind when he kisses her stomach.

Sunshine through the blinds gets Girl's nose itching with the rememberings of burning bacon and the lemon her mama squirts in Girl's eyes, her mama claiming she's trying to add a little kick to her tea. At least, Girl likes to believe every time her mama stings her eyes is an accident but knows memories can shift and turn into pleasant bits to hide away.

One thing Girl knows for sure: Her mama left three years ago, when Girl was six, between putting the bacon on the stove and kissing Girl's forehead good morning.

In Girl's rememberings, her mama brushes curls slick with sleep-sweat from Girl's forehead. Lips press hard on Girl's skin trying to reach bone. The crack of her mama's voice like trees breaking from the root when she promises Girl will understand someday.

How her mama disappears in the smoke just before it sets off the alarm.

Girl's daddy is balled fist, spit flying fury as he chases after her mama. Girl waves to her from the doorway, her daddy clinging to the handle of the red pickup truck with rusted popped pimples saying *You ain't shit without me.*

Murmuring *You promised things would be different.*

All while Girl keeps on waving, waiting for her mama to wave back.

Sunshine through the blinds pricks Girl's skin like stepping on her daddy's clipped toenails embedded in the hall carpet. Girl is nine and looks like her mama. That's what her daddy shouts when she runs from flying beer cans.

What her mama might say if she came back.

Since her mama left, Girl is her daddy's Mama, cleaning up his mess just so he can make more mess. Puts jam on both sides of his toasts, learns to scramble eggs, but never how to crisp bacon.

They are sausage people now.

Sunshine through the blinds tastes like something Girl never wants. Something hot, making her taste buds rise in rebellion. Something familiar that she can't shake, like these days living with her daddy in a routine she's tired of repeating but doesn't know how to stop.

Mornings are for cooking and trying to remember her mama's fading face while Girl stares at her reflection in the window. For pretending not to hear her daddy cry for the woman he loves and the bitch that left.

Afternoons are for cleaning up the aftermath of her daddy's sorrows and tantrums.

Evenings are for chats about nothing. For beers, cigarettes, Big Red gum, and the smell of cinnamon before bed.

Nights are for her daddy's best friend and cricket songs. For lowered blinds, rememberings of her mama's kisses and aching arms waving goodbye.

For broken bodies waiting for that sunshine through the blinds.

Plague

A girl fills her father's mouth with dirt. *So the worms will accept him,* she says to the Body Collector standing beside her sobbing mother. *It's time*, her mother says while the girl presses soil beneath her father's nails with a pin. *Sweetie, it's time*, and the girl begs for five more minutes. *Just five more minutes*, she says.

*

The Body Collector rings an old church bell when the fog is heavy at night. *The bells*, whisper the villagers, *can you hear the bells?* They leave the dead on their stoops. Fling the corpses over horsebacks or into the Body Collector's cart as it passes. They dangle the bodies from poles with makeshift hooks attached from the highest windows in their homes.

*

I wish you'd be more careful, says the Body Collector's husband, The Executioner, while cleaning blood from his axe. The Body Collector teases the ends of the Executioner's hood, kisses the oval cutouts of his eyes. *You don't have to go*, he says, and the Body Collector kisses where she imagines his lips might be through his mask. *But I do*, she says, and leaves before he can respond.

Before she can remember the last time she saw the Executioner's face.

*

A man dangles the body of his son from a metal hook attached to an old broom. The Body Collector reaches for the boy. The villagers gather around her. *Let go*, she says. The father pulls the old broomstick closer to his body. *I—I can't*, he says, and the Body Collector stretches. She grabs the boy by his foot. She pulls, watches the father lean out his window, lean into her tugging from below. The Body Collector watches the villagers step back. The broomstick breaks. The boy falls into the arms of the Body Collector.

*

They call it a guillotine, the Executioner says, placing a miniature model on their kitchen table. He slices carrots from The Body Collector's garden. An overgrown fingernail. The fraying ends of his favorite rope. *I'm being replaced,* whispers the Executioner, his hooded head lowering until it rests in his trembling palms. *Who am I,* he says, *who am I if not—*

The Body Collector takes the mini-guillotine from her husband. Tosses it into the fire. They hold each other and watch the wood burn. Watch the metal blade turn red.

*

Three siblings wander the streets at night asking strangers, *Are you our family?* They are covered in boils. They cough and choke on air. They hold hands until they can no longer walk. Ask after their mother, their father, or maybe an uncle, until they can no longer ignore the burning of their eyes. Of their bodies, crouched and trembling. Until they can no longer ignore the sounds of the Body Collector's bell or her hands finding them in the dark.

*

The King summons the Executioner. The King summons the Body Collector. *Do something,* he says, and points towards the royal chambers. The Queen is a sweat stain swaddled in her sheets surrounded by her servants. *I'm here*, says the Queen. The Physician peels a leech from her arm. *Let me sit up,* says the Queen. Her lady-in-waiting dabs her forehead with a wet cloth. The Queen struggles to rise, groans, sinks back into her bed. *Tomorrow*, says the Queen's lady-in-waiting. *We'll try again tomorrow.*

The smell, says the King, nose covered by a handkerchief, *I can't stand the smell.*

*

The Body Collector remembers where all the bodies are buried. Their last words, how they died, if their families still visit their graves. She wonders what will become of her body. What her last words will be. If the Executioner will visit her, if he will still be wearing his hood. *Let me see your face*, she says while the Executioner slides on his boots. *No*, he says facing away from her, *not yet. Not now.* The Body Collector wraps her arms around his waist, kisses the bones that form his spine.

*

The King calls for a public execution. *The center of attention,* he says taking his seat beside the Body Collector in his booth overlooking the crowd. The Queen's favorite servants are led through the crowd by the King's knights, iron shackles keeping them in line. The Queen's physician is next followed by The Queen's lady-in-waiting. The Queen grasps the Executioner's arm. the Body Collector stands to get a better view, to watch the Executioner escort The Queen onto the wooden platform. *On your knees,* says the King. The servants drop. The physician drops. The Queen's lady-in-waiting removes her bonnet, curtsies to the crowd on the way down to her knees. The Queen leans against the guillotine. *I will not*, she says.

The King stands beside the Body Collector and raises his hand. The Body Collector watches the Executioner raise his axe. Watches the heads of the servants disappear into the crowd. Watches someone catch the head of the physician. Hears the Queen yell, get up! to her lady-in-waiting. The Body Collector searches for her husband's eyes within the Executioner's mask. Feels the wind pass when the King lowers his hand. Hears The Queen's lady-in-waiting say *I will not.*

*

The Body Collector throws the Executioner's clothes into the fire. Take off your mask, she says, and he turns away from her. *I can't,* he says, *you know I can't,* and the Body Collector steps closer to the fire, tries to remember the last time she saw her husband's face.

Popcorn Kernel Girl

From within the shell of a popcorn kernel, a little girl sprouts her wings. They are Q-tips small, and the newborn girl can easily curl within a thimble. Her parents, always hoping for a child of their own, light a candle in celebration.

By noon, the girl is a toddler, threatening to wander right off the counter. Father sets up barriers made of towels while mother coaxes her away from the edge with jelly beans and cake crumbs.

At 2 o'clock, the girl is a teenager, pinging against the windows. Father fears she might need glasses while mother worries she might be part fly. But the girl demands to be set free, that her parents just don't understand her. She has needs, and wants, and she's old enough to make her own decisions despite what her parents might think.

At 3 o'clock, Mother holds the teenaged girl by her wings and tells the girl she's grounded. Father promises that their daughter will grow out of it, that this is all just a phase, but Mother still has her doubts.

At 4 o'clock, the girl turns sixteen and asks Mother if she'll ever meet someone like her.

At 5 o'clock, she's outgrown her thimble.

At 6 o'clock, she turns twenty-one. She sits by the window and flirts with moths and fireflies while her father shops online for a bug zapper. *They understand,* she says, and Mother claims that she does too. *How could you*, says the now 28-year-old woman on the following day, *when all you've ever known is here?*

The woman begs her father to open the window, her wings drooping at her sides. Because he cannot resist her, because he sees the toddler still balancing on the edge of the counter, Father opens the window a crack. Mother brings the woman a scarf, which is actually five pieces of string tied together, to keep the chill at bay. The woman tickles Father's nose, nuzzles into Mother's hand, and flies towards the horizon.

Mother and father watch until there's nothing left of her to see. *Shall we make another?* whispers Mother, tilting her head towards the counter, a single popcorn kernel left behind.

One Last Pirouette

I'm in line at the dry cleaners waiting to see if Ximena can wash the bloodstains from Mya's pink tutu. My phone vibrates in the palm of my hand and I think about answering, but permit my prerecorded voice to do all the talking. The detective—whose name I can't remember but always sounds like he's in the middle of a hiccup—never has the answers I need. If he's not the one leaving me a message, it's probably the woman who never stops sweating, trying to organize another Black Lives Matter protest, with my baby's name plastered on posters and sung in chants she'll never hear. Either way, both of them just want me to list all the facts I can remember from that day, leaving my throat dry.

My eyes catch the Xs marking the lost days on Ximena's calendar hanging below the old television leaning on the edge of its stand. Xs marking every day my baby's not here. I let my eyes follow this trail until I see the circle my baby drew months ago in purple crayon, the center of a flower with green petals, after Ximena promised to come to her recital.

I look away when I hear Ximena's footsteps from the back. She appears between dangling plastic-wrapped clothes, and all I can think about are corpses. How all these clothes are here, hanging and unclaimed because their owners don't need them. Plastic hiding them away like the body bag zipped along my baby's center. Numbered outlines of who their owners are, same as the news reports marking where bullet shells fell around my baby's body.

Lester Holt appears on the television, going over everything happening in the world. I see how many teeth I can count before his lips close to sound out the next word. I don't want Ximena thinking I've just been standing here ignoring my phone, that I don't have anything better to do now that I don't know what to call myself.

Then, I hear it.

Mya Louise Collings, daughter of a single mother, shot, and my baby's face is all over the television screen. I don't know what comes out of my mouth, maybe a yelp or a cry. Ximena is leaning over the counter speaking Spanish to me, which keeps my ears clinging to every word. It's nice, listening to something I don't recognize coming from the mouth of the only person I can talk to.

A new reporter, one I don't recognize, is going through the motions, leaving out that my Mya was in the middle of a pirouette before a bullet pierced her skull. I know because, when I found her, her arms were still raised around her head, fingertips still meeting in the middle.

On the television, the faces of neighbors who've never said two words to me start sharing their sorrows over the death of my daughter. *That poor child, so young. That little girl was always smiling. You hate to think it could happen.* All of them never noticing Slim in the shot, shaking his head and spitting whatever his teeth dig from underneath his fingernails on the dirt behind them.

Stoophead Slim, Mya's nickname for him after she heard me calling him stupid and throwing my good house slipper at his head, is on his regular perch two stoops down from mine, talking out the side of his mouth. He doesn't give much up to the reporter, only says he heard the shots. I try to tell Ximena the whole story, but before I can she's holding my hand and nodding. Like she knows Slim was the one who broke the door down, saw me cradling my child's body, and had enough sense to grab my phone from my purse and call the cops. That Slim stepped in when no one else did while the little body in my arms became cold and firm.

Mya had been practicing her pirouettes. Sent me out of the room so I wouldn't see. *No spoilers, Mommy,* was the last thing she said.

Stoophead Slim is replaced by news of rising gas prices. Ximena understands the words I don't need to say. I can tell by the way her tongue clicks after flicking the roof of her mouth, and she says something else in Spanish. I know from her tone and the way her free hand is moving she's cussing that reporter out.

She never lets me go, even while she's looking for the remote, she's still holding my hand.

"How long—." I still can't say *before my baby's blood stain is gone.*

"There was a lot. Too much." Ximena keeps her eyes on the television. "Maybe you—."

I tighten my grip on her hand to get her to stop. To keep myself standing. Mya was in the middle of a pirouette. Practicing to be perfect.

Ximena's thumb is swiping away all my tears and, though I try to lower my head, she keeps it raised and facing her.

"I will fix." She lets go of my hand and disappears into the back.

My eyes shift from the television back to the calendar and I try to remember all the dates that mattered in the rhythms Ximena used to swipe those Xs on days that are gone. I remember meeting the man I loved for a day, peeing on a pregnancy test in the subway, telling my mother I was pregnant, holding her when she cried. Giving birth to Mya. Mya learning to crawl, run, walk. Her first ballet class. My mother dying. Explaining what death means to my child. Mya's sixth birthday.

And today, a purple circle with green petals, my baby's last drawing.

"Ximena?" No matter how many times I cry for her, my voice keeps stretching past the hanging clothes,

Call Me Verdean

I move to the third level of a parking garage after someone shoots a bullet through my cheeks. I can still taste the metallic tang of the bullet, my tongue tracing the holes it left behind. My life's not so bad in the garage, at least, I don't think it is. I don't remember my life before the craving for brains set in. I've got it under control now, not like before when visitors were common.

People would stop by my garage all the time and break things that weren't theirs. They, technically, weren't mine, either, but I worked hard to make this garage a home. Then, here come the people, with their bats and crowbars, breaking windows and leaving glass on my floors. Stepping on shattered glass—barefoot—really hurts, undead or not. I think that's what they call me, undead, though I don't feel all that dead.

I know they call me ohno whenever they see me. The people are always screaming "Ohno" and yes, hello, hi, but also, I have sensitive ears and you're leaving glass everywhere, so could you please just leave me alone? At least, I'd like to say all of this, but words just don't come easy for me. One moment you think you're having a conversation with a home invader, and the next, you're snacking on their brains.

Not that you meant to, I never mean to, but brains smell like burning leaves and lemon. I don't know how I remember those smells, but when I bite into a person's head, that scent just seeps out, and the voices screaming Ohno get just a little quieter.

But that was before I got control of the cravings. Now, the people don't come around as often and, when they do, they travel in packs. I hear them talk about the hordes of the undead, about shelter, about their lives before. I like to pretend I'm part of these conversations. That I'm sitting around their fire barrels, telling them who I am and where I'm from.

I would tell them my name is Verdean. I wouldn't hesitate because that would be suspicious. I wouldn't tell them about my cravings or the snacking on brains, because everyone has a past, and that past doesn't always need to be shared. I would say I've killed five people, a family, that I had no choice in the matter. When observing the people, I've noticed that five seems to be a safe number. One, and you're inexperienced, often pushed forward to be devoured (I won't tell them that I've participated in the devouring). Fifteen, and you're marked as dangerous. Exiled because, clearly, you are capable of taking care of yourself and have no use for a pack. When asked how many of the undead I've killed, I'd say I lost count a long time ago.

No one seems to care about the lives of the undead.

I would tell the people I'm heading to Philadelphia in search of Billy Penn. I heard a woman say this once to a man playing beneath one of the cars on my floor. She talked about Rocky and a cracked bell and a safe haven beneath it all, originally built by Billy Penn. She said if they could make it there, maybe they could start over. Maybe, if I could make it there, Billy Penn would help me start over, too.

I won't tell the people this next part. I'm not proud of what I did. I just wanted to talk to her, to ask her more about Billy Penn. As I approached her, she sneezed, and the man said, "Bless you." I liked how that sounded, so I tried to say "Bless you," too, but even the nicest things get mangled when I try to say them.

The woman screamed what the people call me, Ohno, and the man hit his head on the underbelly of the car. I raised my hands, but somehow that made everything worse. Trying to explain made everything worse, so much worse, because the man threatened me with a crowbar.

I've lost so many friends to crowbars.

I won't tell the people that I tried to explain that my name is Verdean. That I just wanted to reach Billy Penn in Philadelphia. That, when the man kept swinging the crowbar at me, and the woman kept saying Ohno, Ohno, Ohno, no, no, I forgot the point of it all. I didn't give into my craving, but I did shatter a car door window and press hard on its horn.

I watched the man see me for the first time. Acknowledge that I knew what I was doing, that I wouldn't stop, that it was too late for the both of us. He grabbed the woman's arm, she was now crying Ohno, and they ran, but that didn't matter. I took my hand off the horn, but that didn't matter, either.

I'll ask the people how to get to Philadelphia, that I wish I could've saved the family of five, which was actually a family of two. I'll tell the people about Billy Penn, how the mother spoke so highly of him.

How the father did the best he could to protect us all when the horde came. How there was nothing more I could do.

And I'll wish for things like I've heard the people do. How I wish I could hear their voices one last time, wish that things could've been different, wish that I could've done more to protect them, wish that it had been me instead of them even though I know, just like I know these people would call me Ohno instead of Verdean, that there was nothing more I could do.

Pay What You Will
for the Fair Child

I pay five dollars to see you, the boy in the box. You never notice me because, every Saturday, I sit in the back row on a brown metal folding chair waiting for someone to wheel you on stage. Today's your final performance in town and that's why, I assume, the crowd is bigger than usual. This is my first time seeing you like this, always forced to watch people disappear within the tents of the fairgrounds from across the gravel road. People who don't think of five dollars as being a meal, some thread to stitch a hole. Five dollars to keep Daddy in the present.

The crowd hushes when you appear with a red cape draped over your box. A man, not like Daddy, waves his hands and tells us your story.

The boy in the box, found on the sands of Tortuga, tucked away in a pirate's forgotten treasure!

I don't know where Tortuga is, but I like the sound of pirates. Those who take to the sea for adventure following maps and rumors and intuition stolen by rum. Pirates, who take whatever they want, never caring about what they need. Never caring about who they used to be.

The man finishes his speech and removes the cloak. I miss seeing you, your figure swallowed by everyone who stands and gasps. The sight of you causes a woman to faint. I think something has shattered, a tiny explosion I can't hear, because so many colors fill the tent and all the other children reach for them. I stand on my chair, convincing myself that these lights are fairies, though I thought I had outgrown such things. But they're not, because these lights are you, and this truth causes the adults to weep.

You are crouched and curled within a box we can all see through wearing nothing but shards of glass. Your head is turned away from the men, women, children, me, and all you offer is your sharpened shoulders. Your hair is cut so short I can barely see your furious curls. The bottoms of your feet still peek beneath your dark skin, and I wonder if they are still as soft as the day you were born.

When the man taps your box, you roll within your container, until your head presses against the top of its surface. I decide it's better Daddy didn't come; you look so much like him from the side. Besides, I couldn't afford the extra ticket and can't afford him knowing what's become of you.

We take our seats and the man asks if we have any questions for the boy in the glass box. A woman asks how you eat and you slip your lips between a widened hole and swallow air like a fish. A man wonders if you can do a full rotation in the box, and you do, once, twice, six times, making the lights dance again. A child wants to know your favorite color, favorite fruit, if fairies truly exist?

The man tells the child to ask one question at a time, that five dollars won't cover that many thoughts. The adults laugh and the children imitate their sounds while I slip off my chair. I can't afford to see you, to ask you something I can take home.

The child asks, what happened to his family?

I believe the man will dismiss the question, but instead he chooses to answer. He removes a yellow cloth from his pocket, dabs his eyes, blows his nose.

A very sad story, dear child, he says *The boy has no family left.*

And you curl yourself tighter as if this is true, your body becoming smaller in the box. I pull myself onto my metal chair and curl myself as you do. Perhaps they would call me the fair child in the folding chair, though I'm not fair and can't imagine being bound here. I know I'd want my price to be pay what you can so Daddy could come when he could. So Mama would come without any shame, be impressed by how I can fold my limbs, my head, my toes into this chair, and I'd tell her I learned all this from you.

You, the boy in the glass box, who left me with Daddy. Who left me and Mama before Mama left, too, perhaps to go to Tortuga and be trapped by pirates?

I don't remember raising my hand or deciding to stand on my chair, but the man is pointing at me. I ask the only question I can think of, the only thing I can hope to take home.

What's his name?

For the first time, you face the crowd, and I see you still carry my eyes. I named you before Mama and Daddy could, claimed you, because when you took your first look around the world, your eyes only held me.

His name is Jack, and the man asks if there are any more questions, and, though there are, you never let me go.

What must you think of me, wearing a dress made of the clothes you left behind? Hair cut short like yours and sold for a few extra coins? Scarred hands from doing the jobs of men, pressing myself into tight spaces? I suppose we still have that in common, you in your box for the world to see, and me in the crevices no one else can fit, wishing I could be a fair child like you.

Dreaming I could produce fairies from the shattered remains of a life abandoned twice.

For the Love
of Gertrude Stein

My gerbil, Gertrude Stein, hates sunflower seeds, my girlfriend, and when I wear my hair up. She's on a strict diet of bread crumbs and Boston lettuce leaves. Enjoys spending her afternoons napping in my curls and helped me collect all of my girlfriend's things— her clothes, favorite snacks, and other miscellaneous things acquired between dates, kisses, and whispered *I love yous*—and put them in a box labeled "Bye."

And sipped on my tears while monitoring my phone, deleting text and blocking calls from the girl who is now my ex-girlfriend.

My gerbil, who I named Gertrude Stein, loves going to the museum early in the morning, spending hours staring at paintings by people of color. Since she is a gerbil of color, black except her white paws and a white spot on her tummy, she can identify with the topics these artists portray the most. Horace Pippin is her favorite and, should I get another gerbil, she demands I name him Horace Pippin.

Gertrude Stein—she's my gerbil—is best friends with the mouse living in my cupboard, which is not really OK with me because all my Cheez-Its and tea bags have bite marks on their corners. The mouse, her name is Toklas, spends her evenings with Gertrude Stein. They lounge on my bed and cuddle and kiss—so I'm not really sure if they're best friends or not—and watch their favorite movie, *Ratatouille.*

My gerbil, Gertrude Stein, loves me the most even though she nips my fingers when I brush her fur the wrong way or squeaks in my ear when—just the night before—I told her I wanted to sleep in. Who *now* goes to the museum with Toklas and *now* prefers the works of Frida Kahlo.

Gertrude Stein, who is my gerbil, runs in circles on my chest one morning, panicked because Toklas is gone. I scratch behind her ear to soothe her, use my pinky to catch her tears and allow my darling gerbil to nap within my curls.

When my gerbil, Gertrude Stein, is curled into herself and snoring, I tuck her in my bed before going into my kitchen. In my cupboard, I recover my Cheez-It box where Toklas' upturned body lies and hope it's not too late—since today's trash day—to leave her on the curb.

My Exes Show Up to Your Funeral While All I'm Craving Is a Sunkist

Dr Pepper

I categorize my exes by soda brands. You, a Sunkist. An unexpected choice that still lingers on my tongue despite the years we've missed each other. Him, a Dr Pepper, biting my tongue every time we kissed, somehow sensing you on my breath. I didn't invite him to your funeral. Didn't ask him to escort me down the aisle to your open casket. He understands when I can't make it to you. Helps me to the last pew by the door.

Sprite

I don't recognize him at first. One minute I'm sitting next to Dr Pepper, and the next I'm sipping on the condolences of a Sprite. The *thank yous* dance in the back of my throat, forming burps I try to swallow. You used to say Sprite goes with everything, and once, I believed you. His *I'm sorrys* turn into *Don't you remembers*, and I'd like to say yes, I do. Yes, you paired well with Passion Fruit Pirate Bay. Yes, that one time on the beach before sand and the salt of the ocean seeped into all the crevices I didn't know I contained. Yes, you were always terrible at being alone.

Mellow Yello

I've moved up three pews by the time he walks in. Pretends to weep over your body. Replaces your pocket square with a tiny green leaf and laughs at his own joke. We made the decision to use each other. I used him as a substitute for you. He wanted someone who craved him, who could make him believe he could ever be their first choice. You would've laughed at my theatrics, joked about giving me an Academy Award. For best comedy, best actress in a limited series, best overall performance, best unique and artistic production.

Coke

He finds me stranded in the aisle. *A real shame*, his words fizz in my nose. He talks about you. He talks about me talking about you, our stories becoming his. Our time on the lake in a canoe we carved from a log. Listening to a summer storm throw branches on the roof. *I was never good enough.* I'm happy he knows. I'm happy he says it even when he reaches for my hand. *Not* ... in front of you? Would you care, even now, if I dared to have another taste?

Diet Pepsi

Your fingers are like popsicle sticks. I can't face the rest of you. Try to run and I'm in his arms. Still strong, still safe. Still there despite everything I've done. Called him by your name in and out of bed. Made sure he knew we'd never be anything more than the casual fling until I dropped the word "fling" when he wanted something other than "casual." He promised to be better than you, and in some ways he was. But every time I believed I preferred his kiss to yours, I'd lick my lips and find you lingering there.

Ginger Ale

I'm at your side. I'm straightening your orange tie. I'm rolling the leaf Mellow Yello left behind like a joint and tucking it behind my ear. I'm avoiding touching your skin. I'm waiting for your chest to rise, for your eyes to open, for you to say that I've found you. That this was all just a game. I don't realize I'm crying until my tear falls on someone else's hand. Until I wipe my cheek, find that it's damp, and a voice says *Take all the time you need.* I never knew I could. You never gave me the option. Though his hand is gone, I know he's behind me, the warmth on my skin familiar. I kiss you goodbye. I kiss you in hopes that I was one of your final thoughts. I kiss you, knowing this will be the final time, hoping that the flavor of me still remains on your dying tastebuds.

Fortune's Wish

Nandi glances over multiplication problems and unfinished graphs while turning to Chapter 24. Tucked in her textbook's seam is a cootie catcher with worn edges, its surface split into four color-coded squares: red, blue, green, and yellow.

During recess, she shows the cootie catcher to her best friend, Ese, who swipes the paper toy and brings it to life, small hands flapping its mouth. Shasta—a cautious girl who chews on her collar when nervous, bored, or tired—reaches for Nandi's textbook instead.

"Look," Nandi rests her chin on Shasta's shoulder. The names of the textbook's previous owners are all listed in Sharpie, some with heart-dotted Is some underlined three or four times, some barely there. "All girls."

"Who cares?" Ese says.

And, because Ese doesn't care, Nandi suddenly doesn't care, either. "Let's play."

"I'll go first."

Nandi sits in front of Ese while Shasta traces each name. Nandi picks the color blue, the number two, eight, and four.

"What's it say?" Nandi leans forward, her nails digging into her bare knees. Even Shasta looks up from the textbook to watch Ese peel back the triangle flap revealing Nandi's fortune.

"You will marry at 19."

"That's it?" But Nandi can tell Ese's upset.

Ese is never quiet.

Shasta closes the textbook and looks at the fortune. She chews on the collar of her uniform and then withdraws it, the spit soaking through. Her blue eyes meet Nandi's.

"What?"

You will marry appears on Nandi's triangle fortune followed by 19 written in someone else's handwriting. But the words, *you will marry*, appear over and over again. *You will marry, you will marry, you will marry,* until they blend into one.

Ese bounces back from her momentary silence, claiming that Nandi is just unlucky. This is also why Shasta is left in charge of telling Ese her fortune.

"You will have many children."

Nandi holds Ese's hand, witnessing her best friend's face crumble, an eyelash falling on her cheek.

Ese doesn't like children.

Shasta continues the game, opens a triangle flap to reveal her fortune. "I'll become an old maid, *forever alone*."

All three read Shasta's triangle together, chanting forever alone, the words sinking to the cootie catcher's center.

"This can't be right." Ese throws the cootie catcher across the room. "These fortunes are lame."

"Are they?" Nandi surprises herself. She has never questioned Ese.

"Did you know that the cootie catcher was originally called the salt cellar?" Shasta whispers into the wet spot of her collar. "It was meant to be a container that—"

"Nobody cares!" Nandi says louder than she means to. When Shasta burrows her face behind her damp collar, Nandi bites her tongue.

Ese rolls her eyes at Shasta before turning her attention to Nandi. "You *want* to get married?"

"You don't?" Nandi says.

Ese thinks about this. "Maybe. I don't know."

"Maybe she'll be nice." Nandi smiles, thoughts of what her future wife might look like causing her palms to sweat.

"Maybe *she* will be a *he*." Ese pinches Nandi's elbow.

"We should put it back," Shasta murmurs, retrieving the cootie catcher from underneath a classmate's desk.

"We should throw it away," Nandi adds despite opening her textbook to Chapter 24.

"We should burn it." Ese moves away from Nandi and Shasta, who return the cootie catcher to its crease.

"What do you think the others got?"

Shasta holds herself, her question left to linger between the three of them. Nandi looks to Ese for an answer but receives a shrug and averted eyes. This was supposed to be fun, Nandi thinks, approaching Ese with the same caution she approaches Shasta after school when they practice kissing while waiting for the bus. She plucks the fallen eyelash from Ese's cheek.

"We can make things right with a wish."

"All of us?" Shasta asks.

Ese takes her eyelash back. "Yes and whoever has the worst fortune, their wish will come true."

They close their eyes, each making a wish. One girl wishes to have her fortune erased. Another wishes to make a slight edit to hers. One pleads for the fortune of another.

They go to the window and Shasta unlocks the latch. Nandi presses her palms against the glass and forces the window open. Ese ensures her finger is outside, dangling just over the sill, and blows. All three girls watch the eyelash carry their wishes into the distance, to someone who might grant them.

"What now?" Nandi checks the clock: Five more minutes until recess is over.

"Now," Ese opens the textbook to the page where the previous owners are listed, "we add our names to the book.

Nandi hesitates. What if writing our names spoils our wishes? she thinks. But Shasta has already retrieved a Sharpie from her desk.

Ese steals it and writes her name first, putting two dots for eyes inside the lowercase E's center.

Shasta writes her name in perfect cursive, causing Ese to scoff and shake the desk, which gives Shasta's "T" an extra-long tail.

They both look to Nandi.

"Why?"

"Because they did it." Ese tilts her head to the list of names. "There must be something to writing your name down in the book."

Shasta takes Nandi's hand in hers, slips the Sharpie into her palm. "Trust us, Nandi."

Shasta's hands are so warm, Nandi allows herself to stay in their grasp for a while.

"Come on," Ese taps her foot.

Nandi adds her name, no heart over the lowercase I, no flourishes, just *Nandi* in her stilted handwriting.

"Now to get rid of the book." Nandi turns back to Chapter 24, runs her finger along the edge of the cootie catcher still tucked within the seam.

Ese and Shasta nod, their hands on Nandi's shoulders.

Nandi slams the book closed and takes it to the lost and found. She wraps it in an old sweater and buries it beneath a deflated football, some tattered workbooks, and muddy cleats.

Something Between Them

A knife lies between the woman and the mouse.

The woman drums the tips of her fingers upon the surface of her kitchen table, a gift from her mother, who buries cigarette butts in the pots where the woman plants her tulips. She imagines the fires her mother starts, the way the roots curl and evaporate beneath poisoned soil while smoke rises and the woman wonders, if a mouse is caught in a fire, would their heart rate remain the same with so many ways to escape?

Or would it increase, sensing impending death?

Three hundred ten beats per minute.

The mouse, Mrs. Crumb, sniffs the air for the piece of cheese she abandons her home for. A tiny hole she worked hours, in mouse time of course, to carve behind the woman's bed. Mrs. Crumb thinks of her triplets, who she and her husband, Mr. Crumb, lovingly called their mouselings. Thinks back to her mouselings the day before, cuddled on a piece of cloth that she and her husband nipped from an orange dress with white flowers left by a woman, not this woman, but one who smelled of sangria and

169

peppermint. Their little hearts beating 310 beats per minute, increased to 840 beats per minute when the man saw Mr. Crumb skitter from their hole, ready to nip another piece of the dress to perhaps make a blanket. Mrs. Crumb only knows her husband always wanted more no matter the risk, gripping the dress between his paws.

Mrs. Crumb struggled to hear her husband's *I love you* squeaks mixed within the other woman's screams, the way the dress's skirt flared as it soared through the air, stealing Mr. Crumb away.

The woman, before she encounters Mrs. Crumb, found the orange dress under her bed while she cleaned, held it to her body, and traced the white petals and the jagged edges of the bit of cloth missing from the skirt. Noticed how the waist was too small. She threw the dress on her bed, retreated to the kitchen for a snack and to think of better things. Sliced cheese squares on Ritz crackers, the meal her father prepared for nights her mother preferred to spend with other men in other places.

That's when the woman sees Mrs. Crumb standing on her kitchen table and thinks back upon her reflection. Looks past the beauty of the white petals and focuses on the orange poking through. The woman can't stand the color orange and repeats every conversation with her husband reminding him of this simple fact.

Mrs. Crumb sees how the woman trembles, the same way she did watching Mr. Crumb form an arc over the bed, his small body hitting the opposite wall. Remembers how her own body shivered hearing Mr. Crumb's bones shatter, his body a small heap on the floor for the man to sweep into a dustpan and throw away.

The same man they both know should be returning home soon.

And a knife lies between them.

Shoaling

There are piranhas in the water. Swarming until I can't breathe. Until they peel my skin from me, leaving me with the bones and decay of the dead skin they discard.

*

I live in a hollow with glass windows tinted green. Where my voice is mine and does not change and I am the me I want to be.

*

My father is the stingray that killed Steve Irwin because no one likes to be caught off guard. He apologized but was still charged with murder. Some say wrong place, wrong time. Others say just another Sting ray, another statistic. No one asks what I say.

*

Piranhas prey on the weak while sharks watch. I wonder if piranhas grow into sharks or if sharks eat piranhas. I lose count of all the teeth biting into me, all the eyes glowing in the depths at the sounds of my screams.

*

My mother is a dolphin at the worst of times.

*

I stay in my hollow until my bladder breaks, but plenty of fish pee in the ocean so why can't I?
*

Today, I'm an octopus, a brain in each of my arms. This brain is for culture, this brain is for patience, this brain is for silence, this brain is for awareness, and I turn off the rest. The rest don't matter, not to the piranhas, sharks, and killers.
*

My mother is an eel at the best of times.
*

I'd rather be a penguin but even they have to come up for air.
*

My mother, the eel, says I should grow a shell. I go into my hollow and emerge as a sea snail. *That's not what I meant*, she says, but it doesn't matter because now my hollow is portable.
*

Piranhas gnaw until their teeth break. Sharks swarm until they're bored. Killers lurk in the depths disguised as whales until I'm caught in their light lures and confronted by anglers.
*

My mother, the dolphin, tears up the note from the anglers about my early dismissal and I want to talk about the piranhas and sharks. But she dances circles around me until I feel like the clown fish I really am.
*

Piranhas love a good joke, especially one that causes the sharks to frenzy. Too bad the joke's on me and my black stripes, but at least I walk away with my skin.

*

The sharks took my hollow and now I'm a blowfish floating fat and upside down surrounded by Piranhas laughing.

*

Remember yourself at all times.
The last words my father said to me before he killed Steve Irwin.

*

Goldfish have two-second memories, which is why so many of them are crackers.

*

The anglers don't appreciate my use of "cracker," but they've never emerged for what the piranhas and sharks call me.

*

My hollow is in my mother's flippers because today, she's putting on a show. She balances my hollow on the tip of her nose, flips it, and rolls it along her silver body. Nose to head. Head to tail. Giggles and tells me I'll be fine without it. Time to grow up, don't listen to the others. Smile until it's over.

*

I'm a bottom feeder and should know my place by now.

*

I swam too close to the piranhas, and one clipped my fin. Another brought me to the surface while the sharks stood by and watched. I don't remember what it felt like to stop breathing while someone filmed. Only that bits of my fin floated away from me while the sun burned my scales.

*

Fish taste best fried.

*

My mother is an eel and I am a croaker and together we surround the Anglers. But we have no proof except my damaged fin and can't afford to fight the swarm.

*

I'm allowed to rebuild my hollow where I practice becoming an eel. I stretch and throw electricity, but away from my hollow, I'm a shrimp.

*

Piranhas don't like being called out and proceed to let me know so. One day, they leave the bones of their meals in my desk. Swim into me on purpose. Block my path, nip at my scales, make up reasons for the sharks to come. I can feel my hollow breaking, and I'm starting to think I won't mind when it eventually shatters.

*

My mother has remained an eel.

*

I grab the piranha who clipped my fin and drag it to the surface. It screams and fights but the others just watch, except the one who films the whole thing. The sharks circle but still they just watch, and I drop the siranha and keep swimming towards the surface until I can feel the sun searing my scales.

*

I am a salmon leaping over river falls and between the teeth of bears.

*

I will never be an eel. Not an angler or a shark or a piranha. Two seconds and they won't even remember me.

But I will always remember them.

My Dead Sister Looks Good on Me

My sister dies on the last day of fall. I remember the colors of the leaves, the crunch of the fallen ones under my shoes as I walked out of the hospital alone. The smoke that left me when I opened my mouth. The scream that followed. The feel of my tears as they dampened my scarf, the blare of a taxi's horn.

The morning of my sister's funeral, the ground is covered with frost. My father doesn't shower. My sister's husband stands outside our front door. My mother makes peanut brittle, just in case. I stand in our old bedroom, staring out the window we used to share. Staring at my dead sister's husband standing outside our front door. My father doesn't shave. My mother makes three loaves of bread, just in case. My sister's husband doesn't come inside when I answer the door. *I can't*, he says and walks to his car. We let our bodies do the rest.

We all cry when they lower my sister into the ground. *She wanted to be cremated*, I say but no one listens to me. I'm used to being the other child, the one who was good while my sister was great. We received the same grades but she was first chair violin. I was valedictorian but only because my sister had her degree mailed to her while building self-sustaining water structures in the Amazon. My sister, the adventurer, the wife to a husband she saved from underground fight clubs. The daughter my parents called every day instead of once a week.

I sleep in the room we used to share after her death. Move back home after the third call from my landlord about rent. Get a job at Whole Foods. Find all the things my sister left: hair dryer, books, her violin, a little red book with the phone numbers of her exes, clothes, sheet music, her lipstick, a compact mirror.

One day, while my mother is in the cupcake phase of her grief, I try on my dead sister's lipstick. *That's a nice color on you*, my mother says and I nod, say, *I'm trying something different*. I start wearing my dead sister's clothes. First her socks, a headband or hat. Her skirts. Her dresses. I lose weight to fit into her pants. Read her books. I take lessons and learn how to play the violin. Learn to copy her handwriting through sheet music and the cell phone numbers of her exes. I play until my teacher says, *There's nothing else I can do*. Hear my father say, *Beautiful*, while I'm playing "Your Song" by Elton John on my sister's violin.

I dye my hair, style it like she did. While my mother is in the pie phase of her grief, I quit my job at Whole Foods. Try out for the orchestra, get in, but not first chair. I call my sister's exes. Leave voicemails telling them the good news. Say, *It's a start. Say, I miss you. Call me when you can.* And they do. They all do. Some angry, some sad, some married or lonely or drunk or locked in their closets saying, *I'm hiding from my kids.*

I tell my sister's exes that ending the relationship was for the best. Some tell me how it ended. Some agree and let the conversation die. Some ask me questions I can't answer. About my sister, about us, about time wasted or time they've spent waiting. Some ask about my life, how I'm doing, how I've been. I say that I'm married, even though I'm not. I'm happy, which I doubt. I just wanted to check in which is true. I hang up, no matter how they try to answer.

My mother stops baking when she calls me by my sister's name. My father takes long showers that warp the bathroom walls. Shaves. Buys a dog that sleeps in my room. A dog that howls when I practice for an upcoming concert. A dog that rests his head in my lap, who lifts his head when he notices I've stopped reading. *He likes you*, my father says, and kisses my head. He doesn't say anything about me lounging in what used to be my sister's bed.

I jog in the park, because that's what she used to do. Pull my hair in a tight ponytail, power walk down the hall. *I'm going for a run,* she'd say, then jog the entire time. This is how my sister met her husband, how I meet her husband. I smile her smile, keep pace with his pace. Recognize the smile he flashes before tucking it away.

The smile he gave my sister.

You look different, he says and I smile the smile my sister would give him. I tell him I've changed. Tell him about starting over. How I've reached out to my exes. Started playing violin. When we break for water, I pull out my sister's lipstick. *That color,* he says while I rub my lips together.

You don't like it? I tilt my head towards him, make sure the eyes that match my sister's catch the sun so he can see how much I want him.

No, he says.

I mean yes, he says. *Yes, I like it.*

And I run. I run how she would run. The taste of my sister's lipstick on my teeth. I hear her husband follow. Feel his breath on my shoulder. Watch him run by my side. *It looks good on you*, he says, and I tell him my sister's name.

Whisper it, like she did, the first time.

A Lethal Woman

I am the femme fatale. I linger in doorways, knee bent, back of my hand pressed to my forehead. I cry in camera light. Tears shining, lips quivering, but my mascara never runs. My blush always accentuates my cheeks. I always fall for the detective, even though I ask him to solve the case of my murdered husband. To find my missing jewels. To help me because I am a helpless woman in need of protection. In need of saving. In need of a man. I am a portrait captured in black and white. A woman absent of color despite my pencil skirts and blazers that caress my curves when I walk. The heels that meld to my feet. I learn to run in these heels. How to be kidnapped, how to fight, how to stand perfectly still in these heels with a gun pressed into my temple. I wonder what will it take to be rid of these heels. I run into the arms of the detective in these heels. Kiss his cheek, his lips, allow our foreheads to touch, our noses to rub together because I am ... what? In love? I know this isn't a romance story, just another detective claiming his reward for another case solved. Never mind the bodies. My dead husband. My missing jewels nestled in the detective's safe. Never mind that I cracked the case, identified the murderer, found all the clues while posing in the light. While sitting across from the detective, blinds scarring my face. That I, the femme fatale, guided the detective to the answer with a well-placed trip, a single tear tracing my jawline, a scream that baited him towards the villain, my kidnapper. I know the detective isn't ready for the mysterious case of the swollen ego so—I knock. I knock on the glass pane of a door with his name etched in black letters. His name that pulls the camera's lens in close. No one knows my name, not like they know his. I'll enter because the detective tells me to. Walk in because that's what the detective says, *That's when she walked into my life*, without moving his mouth. Sit across from him, dab at my tears with a handkerchief I didn't know I had. Tell him *I need your help*. Tell him *Please, help me* in a single sigh even though I know how this story ends. I've played this part before, except this time I'll cross my legs. Let the camera capture the blood on my heel. Frame it in black and white so only I know it's there.

It's Been Fun, Madam Miggs

Plaintiff: Mariah Williams
v.
Defendant: Madam Miggs
Complaint for Divorce Filed on:
December 31, 2002

1.The Defendant Admits All Allegations in Paragraph
1. Mariah, you assume—just because you're turning 13 in the coming year—that you'll no longer need me. However, I dare to disagree. Who, mind you, holds your hand during thunderstorms? Who eats the cooked carrots that make your tongue writhe in the back of your throat? Who pretends to be the boring horse so you can be the prettiest unicorn at the ball? I would also like to remind you that I'm the one who planned those elaborate tea parties in the backyard for you and your friends. Not Teddy Ruxpin, who is all thumbs, and definitely not that basic bitch Barbie.

2.The Defendant Denies All Allegations in Paragraph 1.
You don't get to age out of your best friend—

your first friend—just because you meet some taller, pimple-faced kids who know how to apply makeup. You don't need to get rid of your childish things because you don't play with them anymore. We had so much fun playing with your train set every Christmas, didn't we? Don't you remember how we'd spend hours just watching it circle the tree? Don't think I haven't noticed you sneaking your Lite Brite, Bop-It, Moon Shoes, and butterfly clips into the attic for "safekeeping." We both know Betty Spaghetti doesn't do well around spiders. *Where the Wild Things Are* is essential literature and should not be placed in a box marked "Goodwill" with poor Teddy. I could care less about Barbie, but if you've forgotten the fundamental lessons from your childhood, *clearly*, I'm still needed!

3. The Defendant Admits:

I've forgotten the last time we played together. I remember when you didn't mind that the other children couldn't see me. We used to tell each other everything, go everywhere together. Now, you're going to swim meets, hanging out with your new friends, and when I ask if you have time to talk—if you want to spend some time with me—it's always "I'm busy, Miggs." Since when am I just "Miggs" to you? Since when is homework or *Degrassi* or trifolding poster boards or your gel pen collection more important than us? I don't want you to think that I'm starving for your attention. I'm not. Honestly, I've been pretty busy, too. I've been keeping an eye on your room for you, making your bed, cleaning the window where we used to play, I Spy. I hope you know that, no mater how busy

I might be, if your new friends are ever mean to you, that I'll always be where you left me.

4.But Denies/Doesn't Know:

You and me, Mariah? We're not like Jacob and Crispin Cricket. Did you hear? Jacob abandoned Crispin in the lost and found box at his school last week. Then there's our friend, Miranda Mobley. Said her girl, Josey, at least had the decency to say goodbye before pretending Miranda never existed. I know she's hard to look at, with her Fred Flintstone's body, Toucan Sam's head, and clothes stolen from Cap'n Crunch, but don't we all deserve more than that? Miranda believes all children either surrender or divorce their imaginary friends. That it's part of our job to ease into the process, just accept the fact that our kids are growing up. You don't need to remind me that I signed a contract that states, "An imaginary friend is to remain in the life of their child until they are no longer needed." Need I remind you about Furby? That little creep who wouldn't shut up, even after you banished him to the basement? Funny how you blamed his cause of death on faulty batteries just like you did with your Tamagotchi and GigaPet. Can't really tell your new friends that your Neopets died due to faulty batteries, too, can you? I really wanted to avoid any hostilities between us. You were my best friend. However, you know Judge Barbie presides over all imaginary friend court hearings. What happened to best friends forever? To pinky swears? To us? Doesn't any of that mean anything to you anymore? Doesn't our friendship mean anything to you? Don't I?

I Keep My Orgasms
to Myself

I keep my orgasms in an urn, just in case. In case Roger with the gap in his teeth licks a little too hard and I just want the whole thing to end. Our situation relies on him not asking questions, a negotiation down from him not talking at all.

In case I'm watching two girls or two guys or hidden cameras or cartoons or Sims and the moans are grating on my nerves but, somehow, lasting longer than my computer's battery. In case I'm bored or in case I'm not, but why not?

And I tell myself every time I can stop. I don't need to look inside the urn, to pull one or two or more of my orgasms out. Especially tonight, while I'm studying for a final exam I probably should pass. I mean, public speaking should only take practice but my C-minus and I don't have time. Passing the exam would spare me the D which would let me survive another semester, but ...

But I've already removed the lid.

My orgasms all look like me, but naked. Confident, with crossed legs and hair pulled back and hips slightly turned so every stretch mark and layer rolled over layer shows.

"I just wanted one."

"Girl," the weakest of my orgasms grabs the pillow from my bed and holds it between her legs. The others run out of my bedroom, all laughing, all excited and smelling like Cucumber Melon or Warm Vanilla Sugar.

"Just ... get back in the urn."

My weakest orgasm bites her lower lip, drags her body over the pillow. I leave, not because she's stubborn, but because she'll take the longest to finish.

"Hey," my suspect orgasm whispers, peeking from behind my roommate's bedroom door. "Got a minute?"

"I need to pass my exam!"

"You don't *need* anything," my twin orgasms call, one with legs spread in the bathroom while the other is probably squatting over the kitchen sink.

She is.

She washes herself, tugging on the spigot's extendable neck, water hesitating to leave her eyelashes, the tip of her nose, her hardened nipples.

My couch orgasms turn on the TV and fight over which sport has the most sweat, the best ass-cam footage, whether that's football or baseball. Until my remote orgasm does what she does best.

"A little help?" Her legs spread on the back of the couch. I can barely see the power button.

"No," I say to them, to myself. To my counter orgasm and my fruit orgasm poking through the fridge. To my vibrator orgasm digging up dirt in my flower pot where I hid the batteries two hours ago. To my quietest orgasm hiding under the sink and my finger orgasm who stares at me, bored with the whole thing.

"You're not being fair," and I hear a door open even though there is no door. "You deserve this," the chimes of quarters being jostled in someone's pocket "We all do."

The smell of detergent. Of dryer sheets. She hugs me from behind and I feel the warmth of freshly dried clothes. The chill of eyes watching through glass windows replaced by the sweat and vibrations of one machine, two, more.

"The laundromat is closed," I pant without meaning to but it feels good to be out of breath.

My spin cycle orgasm, my strongest orgasm, licks the outside of my ear.

"I have to—"

She holds my hand and that's all it takes for me to follow her. My other orgasms watch as she guides me to the window where I draw the blinds, stare out into the dark.

My spin cycle orgasm removes my shirt and unclasps my bra. Presses my breasts against the cold window.

"Let them see you," she says, and I want them to. Even though there are no lights on in the apartments around us, I can see the faint glow of a TV.

I'm naked with my orgasms. With that one TV screen and whoever might be watching, imagining their eyes flicking towards me, my orgasms trembling between my legs. Some hold my arms, others wrap around my legs until I struggle to hold them all. My spin cycle orgasm never lets me go, her breath hot on my neck, her touch an unpredictable force on my breasts, releasing me moments before the pain settles.

A light reveals a neighbor's bathroom. Another shows a front door opening. A censor light picks up movement. A snap and there's a whole kitchen before me. I wait for their eyes, for them to see me and my orgasms. The thought of just one gaze makes my orgasms hold me tighter. The thought of all of them looking nearly makes me collapse.

"You deserve this," they all say in unison and I can see a new orgasm forming in my reflection. She is running towards me, her hand reaching for me, and I know how much I want to deserve this will always overshadow how much I need this to end.

To the Gentleman Reading 10 Tips for the Grieving Widow Before Diving Back into Dating on His Phone in Barnes & Noble

I don't know what it's like to be a widower, but I'd like to. This may appall you—you look like the kind of man who could be appalled—but I'm a terrible romantic. Romantic in the sense that I want to be loved. Terrible because I don't want that love to be permanent.

I noticed the whisper of a wedding band on your finger. How, while you read, you reach into your breast pocket, trace what's hidden there then swipe up to continue reading. If what you keep hidden there is your wedding ring, please know that I don't mind that you keep it so close to a vital organ. I once left an eyelash named Tony in my eye for a week because I wanted to see if I could work through the pain. Then, to see if I could find him, moving my eye in such a way that Tony would be forced out of hiding.

This is how I would approach you, how I would tell you about Tony. You'd probably ask me something sensible; you seem like someone who others would describe as sensible, locking your phone, your screen going dark. *Is Tony, your eyelash, still there?* and I'd lean into your question, towards you, pretending that I don't know. Pretending I can't feel the dull itch of Tony lurking just out of sight, and I'll later tell myself that I was flirting when I told you to see for yourself.

While you look, I'll notice the shadows under your eyes and assume that you still call for your lost lover. That's all she'll be to me, lost, like you've misplaced her and are just retracing your steps. I wish I knew this feeling, to lose something so important to your way of life that everything else appears to be an interruption. Is that how you'll view me? As another interruptions?

You'll find Tony and take the initiative in removing him from me. You'll use the hand you caressed the object in your pocket to gently press into my eye. I'll ask about your wife, try to sound polite when you say something dismissive like, *It's a long story,* like *I'm sorry for your loss* or *Is she no longer with us?* like any part of this moment was meant to be shared with her.

I'll wonder if you'll think I'm rude because you can tell that I don't care about your lost wife. That you can tell that I want you, not in a permanent way, but in a way that you won't need me to be her.

We'll talk about how you retrieved Tony while lying naked in a bed you never shared with her. We won't hold hands in public because sometimes you call me by her name and sometimes I think about offering up my real name as a consolation prize, but I never do.

We won't share our food or feed each other, and I'll think the world will view us as co-workers rather than the convenient lovers we are. We'll never exchange phone numbers, enjoying the spontaneity of each other until oneday, the spontaneity is gone.

You'll sleep through the night. You'll sleep so deeply that I'll think that I've lost you. I'll pinch your nostrils until you gasp for air, until you sit up and call me by the fake name I've loaned you. You'll ask me for pieces of myself that I'll refuse to give. My phone number, my childhood dreams, my birthday, favorite color, and preference: cats or dogs.

I'll want to give you all these things and I list them off as you sleep. I tell you my name, my birthday, repeat my phone number five times, and wait for you to wake. I wait for you to repeat what I've told you while you've slept through the night, and when you don't, I know that it's not too late for me.

You'll sleep through the night so deeply that you won't even notice I've left you. Before I go, I'll whisper the name of your lost wife, leaving you with the name of the dead on your lips. When you wake, you'll realize what a terrible romantic I am. So terrible that even the slightest hint of my name will be gone.

So terrible that I'll place an eyelash named after you in my eye, find someone new somewhere else, and when he asks for my name while removing this eyelash from me, I'll tell myself I'm flirting when I give him the name of your lost wife instead.

After the Lights Go Out, My Father Starts a Fire, and I Sacrifice My Dolls to the Flame

He asks me why and I tell him it's to help keep the fire going, but really, it's because none of these dolls are mine. Aubrey with her golden curls, Susan with her blue eyes and Betty with her freckles. Missy and Jane and Maggie and Rachel with their thin bodies and lace dresses with frills and the paleness of their skin. I ask Father if we could turn them into candles just as Polly's face melts and her eyes roll to our feet. My father kicks them back into the fire with the toe of his shoe and says probably not, and I think that sounds about right. I throw Mila and Grace into the fire together because they came as a packaged deal, a two-for-one sale from a bargain bin, where all the dolls looked the same. I lean in closer to my father and he tells me about his toys. His green Army men, white cowboys, and astronauts without faces. I tell him I wish these dolls were like me, with dark skin and afro puffs. A doll who likes to wear overalls and collect rocks and bugs and blades of grass tucked away in their pockets. My father and I watch the fire chew on these dolls and the sound hurts my ears. As I stare into the flame, I swear I see Grace, her gray eyes watching me. I tell her goodbye, because she was never mine, never me, and that, perhaps, we never belonged to each other.

Close: A Father/Daughter Breakup Defined

Close (adj): a short distance away

We break up over a Wendy's salad. At least, that's what this feels like, a breakup. I guess fathers can't break up with their daughters. You say things like *Your mother and I* and *It's over* and *You'll be better off* and *I love you, kiddo*. The tips of our shoes touch under the table. We pull soggy lettuce from our mouths at the same time, wipe our damp hands on the thighs of our jeans. *See ya*, you say, and I want to believe you. But I can't. Because you step on my foot before you leave. Because you've already forgotten you're my ride home.

Close (adj): carefully guarded

I remember you in fragments so I can pick and choose what to forget. Like when I'm eight and witness you arguing with mom for the first time. Mom on one side of your bed saying she goes out because you've stopped shaving. You on the side where her imprint evaporated three months prior and relocated to the couch. You stopped shaving because she stopped noticing. She only sees the worst in you. You only berate the best version of her. I wonder where these two versions live. I wonder if either of them has time to tuck me in and whisper goodnight.

Close (adv): in a position so as to be very near to someone or something; with very little space between

Before you leave, but after you stop tucking me in, you teach me about love and all its failures. We are at the Ferris wheel's peak when you say I loved you, once. I ask if you still love me. You talk about how love can be felt for so many useless things. I ask if you still love me. You talk about loving the view. I ask if you still love me. You talk about cheesesteaks and Wendy's salads. Watching icicles melt on the gutter. But do you love me? I move closer until our arms intertwine. Until our legs twist, my foot resting on yours. Dad? Dad, you say, three letters, nothing more. Just like love, you say, as we begin our descent. Just four letters, bookended by an "L" and "e." Nothing more.

Close (adj): denoting a family member who is part of a person's immediate family, typically a parent or sibling

You were the only one who didn't make fun of me for watching *The Land Before Time*. I was nine and changed my name to Littlefoot, walking on all fours. You picked tree stars for me from the tallest cabinet, from the top of the fridge. I was 10 watching *Clifford: The Big Red Dog*, lapping chicken noodle soup from a bowl. You called me your good girl between the ages of 12 and 13. At 14, you tucked me in for the last time. You read *The Little Engine That Could*, your breath smelling like pinecones after it rains.

Close (v): move or cause to move so as to cover an opening

After you leave, I pack what remains into cardboard boxes. I use masking tape. I write the names of rooms I imagine your new house contains. Office. Den. Pantry. All in Sharpie, with maps for where each item should be. In a box marked "kitchen" I write an apology for the absence of all your plates. Mom threw them at the trash collectors. They refused to take the only box she packed. The one containing your marriage license and all the half-torn photos of you. She forgets about the worst of you. Only the sees the worst in me. We talk around each other without you. Her having conversations with lamps and lightbulbs, waiting for me to leave too. Me, talking to all the doors and windows, wanting to leave, knowing I need to stay.

Close (n): the end of an event or of a period of time or activity

Six months and you still haven't come. Your boxes remain by the door. There are bills and empty cabinets. There is Mom watching *Wheel of Fortune*. I miss the sight of boiling water. I miss smoke rising from a pot. I miss pine cones and *Clifford* and tree stars. I miss the sound of you pressing microwave buttons. I apply to five Wendy's in the area. Get hired at three. Work at two. The one closest to Mom, who blames me for destroying her body. Who blames me for her loneliness and everything she hates about you. The one where I last saw you, where I make sure the lettuce leaves are never soggy.

Close (v): bring or come to an end

I find out you're married again through Facebook. Your wife looks like Mom. Despite the wig. Despite her crooked teeth. Despite the way you rest your hands on her stomach. I know I won't hear from you. I know I'll never see you again. Still, I want you to know, I'm waiting for you at Wendy's. I'm a grill cook at the one closest to Mom. I work the window at the Wendy's where I last saw you. I imagine your voice through the speaker in the winter. I ask for your order. You tell me about love. How it hurts. How it breaks. How it dissipates when we least expect it. When the window peels open and I see someone else's father, I still try to imagine they're you. I wonder, if I asked, would they tell me they loved me? Or, was this all just a four-letter word, nothing more?

Define a Good Woman

My doctors tell me I'm depressed because I'm chronically ill. My mother says I'm chronically ill because I'm depressed. My father doesn't believe—or acknowledge—my depression. *You're just tired,* he says. My husband acknowledges my depression too much. *Bad day*, he says holding my hand, rubbing my back, poking and prodding my tightened muscles, searching for any signs of life.

*

Wilma Flintstone washes dishes made of stone with water that shoots from a mammoth's blue trunk. She never questions the amount of nose-dew she spreads on her plates, cups, and knives. Doesn't acknowledge the "ow" that escapes the mammoth when she tugs on his nose too hard. She's a housewife, and the last thing she needs is to acknowledge that her appliances have feelings.

*

I think I'll die in this bed. Not today, but someday, wrapped in fleece sheets covered in Canada Geese.

*

Wilma was supposed to have a baby boy during season three of *The Flintstones* until someone came up with the ideal Flintstone toy for little girls. Imagine Fred's surprise to find Wilma in the baby's room, packing three paychecks worth of clothes and toys.

*

My husband believes my body is made of glass. The slightest touch or harsh word will cause me to splinter and shatter. I tell him I am the rubber stick of a hot glue gun. I bend over toilets, straighten as doctors prescribe new treatments. My body melts when being pushed through MRI machines and wheelchairs, until I'm unrecognizable and adhering to the nearest surface.

*

Wilma doesn't know her best friend and neighbor, Betty Rubble, will adopt a baby boy one season after Fred returns the items meant for their son.

*

My father finds me in bed when he and my mother come to visit. He asks if I'm coming downstairs. I tell him I can't. I have a fever. My legs are swollen. My bones are at war with every muscle in my body. He closes the door. I hear him go downstairs, tell my mother that I'm sleeping.

*

Wilma complains to Fred that the garbage disposal is broken. She balances their sleeping daughter, Pebbles, on her hip, vacuums with one foot, irons with her free hand. *In a minute,* says Fred, rubbing his hands together and smacking his lips, his ritual before devouring his Bronto Burger. Wilma rolls her eyes. Pebbles wakes and starts to cry.

*

My husband and I link arms in the park and I don't shrink away from his touch. I rub my nose into his arm. He laughs and kisses my forehead. We are in college again. In love again.

*

For date night, Fred takes Wilma bowling. At first, she crosses her legs and pouts, complains Fred never thinks about her and what she likes. *Oh, Fred*, she says when he asks if she's having fun. Before Fred apologizes, before Wilma asks Fred if he knows what he's apologizing for, Mr. Slate—Fred's boss—laughs. That's all it takes to send Wilma into a rage. Nobody laughs at her Fred. She grabs his stone ball, tiptoes just like Fred taught her, and releases. *Strike*, she says and smirks at Mr. Slate. She picks up Fred, flings him over her shoulder. Makes him promise to take her dancing next time.

*

My mother sits on the edge of my bed and tells me I have a good man. I tell her I know, and I do know, just like I know I'm not a good woman.

*

Fred exchanges the old garbage disposal for a new one. Wilma kisses his cheek. Pebbles claps and Dino barks, running circles around the whole family. Everyone laughs. The credits play. No one talks about what happens to the now homeless pigasaurus—a purple pig with tusks, black spots, and purple spines running down his back—that's been eating the Flintstone's trash for years.

*

I imagine another woman. How she fills a room with her scent—sometimes pine or bacon. Burning leaves would be her favorite scent. My husband's favorite scent. My imaginary woman wouldn't calculate how long to laugh at a joke, edit her response to *Are you OK?* She just knows things. She knows she is the imaginary woman. Knows how to love my husband, be the daughter my parents miss. She knows I'm upstairs imagining her. My imaginary woman knows that the strength to leave this bed will never find me, that I'll only burrow deeper under the covers.

*

Fred and Wilma Flintstone are one of the first television couples to sleep in the same bed. If you ask Fred, he'll say they were the first animated couple to do so. *Take that, Jetson!* Wilma giggles her signature giggle knowing her husband's secret. That he can only sleep when they're cuddled up together, his arm wrapped around her waist. He knows when she's having a nightmare by the way her body curves and clenches. During those moments, she feels his arm tighten around her, feels his lips find her in the dark.

*

I have settled on a life where I live in this bed. Where my husband crawls in and asks *Can I touch you?* I love the sound of his voice in the dark, how it seeps into my skin. *No* I say, because his voice isn't enough. *Just let me look at you*. We stare at one another until he tells me about his day. Until I tell him I'm sure my father will never understand. How my mother does but doesn't know what to do. I feel his fingers brush against mine. The small *why* that slips from his lips when I pull away. *I can't*, I say. I see my husband's face in the dark. His skin a sheath pulled over bone, eyes searching for a version of me that is trapped in bedsprings. Trapped in something no one can name but keeps me confined to a room with no locks.

Acknowledgments

There are never enough words to express how grateful I am to Michael Czyniejewski, Joel Coltharp, and the Moon City Press team for giving my debut flash fiction collection such a wonderful home. Thank you and Shen Chen Hsieh for creating the cover of my dreams, a reflection of myself that I can keep and carry with me across lifetimes.

Thank you, dear reader, for taking the time to read this collection filled with micros and flash. The book in your hands would not have been possible without the guidance, lessons, and encouragement of others.

Thank you Tara Campbell, Kathy Fish, Cathy Ulrich, Tommy Dean, Chelsea Stickle, Exodus Oktavia Brownlow, Melissa Llanes Brownlee, Lindsey Pharr, Veronica Klash, Cheryl Pappas, Sarah Freligh, Charmaine Wilkerson, Davon Loeb, Kim Magowan, Josh Denslow, Shannon Frost Greenstein, K.C. Mead-Brewer, Jasmine Sawyers, Meg Pokrass, Ruth Joffre, Christina Rosso-Schneider and Alex Schneider, Madeline Anthes, Hannah Grieco, Christopher

Allen, Helen Rye, Jude Higgins, Diane Simmons, Christopher Gonzalez, T.E. Wilderson, Tara Stillions Whitehead, and so many more! I could write an epic filled with thanks to each and every one of you for the workshops you've led, the advice you've given, and your unending support of my strange creations.

Thank you to all my teachers who saw my love of writing and nourished the seed that would eventually grow into this collection and so much more. Pete Duval, Cherise Pollard, Luanne Smith, and my Spalding MFA family. Special thanks to my elementary school teachers, Teacher Betty Peditto and Teacher Angela Di Maria, who continue to support me and my work after all this time.

And Teacher Nancy Adele who provided the original assignment, the creation of a book of poems, that would eventually lead me on the journey to this book and so much more.

Thank you to my trash cat mama, Claudia Love, and my fellow trash cats, Karyl Anne Geary and Lindsey Bee, for your words, memes, and stories. Special thanks to my heavenly trash cat and wifey in writing, Sara Beth Lowe. I wish you could have shared this moment with me but know you always knew it would happen.

Thank you, Dr. Esther Bubb, for making sure my hair always looked fabulous no matter what color. To my forever roomie, Sienna Golden Malik, thank you for always being there for me and my writing even during those terrible drafts in our high school dorm room. Alyssa Shirey for the tarot readings, zodiac chats, and texts about our past, present, and futures! Chelsea McGarity, thank you for all the adventures, for making me laugh even when the ideas weren't there, and for always telling me to send you my stories when the publication date arrived. Thank you, Ashley Duval, for humoring all my crazy ideas, for knowing my angles, and capturing my best sides in 100-degree weather.

To Elizabeth Burton, thank you for the submission parties, draft exchanges, and pushing me to edit. Without you, many of these stories would still be in progress.

My writing partner-in-crime, Annie Frazier, thank you for all the text exchanges, me blurting out ideas as they come and you never sending any of them away, always encouraging me to keep pushing and digging until these ideas become stories. Thank you for being there to keep me grounded whenever I try to fly off into the future, ready for the next big thing when the project in the now isn't moving fast enough. For always telling me great things are on the horizon for me and my writing. I can't wait to talk more about future projects while eating Thai food in the park.

My forever best friend, Megan Colgan: Thank you for the cookies and sushi and dim sum and Rita's and the now multiple failed attempts to dine at Fellini. One day we'll make it! Thank you for getting me out of the house, for reminding me that not all writing has to be done in isolation, and that I need to go exploring (even in the winter) to keep the ideas coming.

All my love to my family, both Buckhaulter and Carle, for your support. For feeding me the best food around and providing the spirits that nestle in the bones of all of my stories.

Thank you, Sherry Jones, for all the visits, discussions about Big Brother, the laughs, support, and for fueling my creativity with delicious apple salad. I'll be over soon to pick up the latest batch.

Thank you to my dad, Ira Carle, for being the logic behind my creativity. For the long car rides where the ideas that sparked the stories came to life. For all the snacks and telling me when it's time to work and when I need to take a break. Thank you for all your advice during this process and for always listening, even when the words don't make sense.

And to my mom, Selena Buckhaulter Carle, thank you. Thank you for being my first reader and editor, and believing that I could get this far and further. For always asking when I need edits back even when there's no deadline. For telling me stories and giving me hugs when those stories don't find their way to the page.

Without the two of you, I wouldn't be the writer, or person, I am today.

Thank you to the editors and readers of the following journals where the listed stories have originally appeared:

"A Lethal Woman" published in *No Contact*

"A Letter to My Breasts" published in *The Offing*

"Abernathy_Resume.docx" published in *Porcupine Literary*

"At the Only Friendly's Open When the World Ends" published in *Cheap Pop*

"At the Risk of Missing My Heart" published in *The Flash Fiction Festival Anthology*, Volume Four

"Bite" published in *Passages North*

"Black Bottom Swamp Bottle Woman" published in *The Rumpus*

"Call Me Verdean" published in *Five South Lit*

"Can I Take Your Order" published in *ASP Bulletin*

"Close: A Father/Daughter Breakup Defined" published in *Moon City Review*

"Dandelion" published in *Milk Candy Review*

"Define a Good Woman" published in *Waxwing Magazine*

"Draft No. 1" published in *Pidgeonholes*

"For the Love of Gertrude Stein" published in *Mineral Lit Mag*

"Fortune's Wish" published in the *2021 Best Short Stories of Philadelphia Anthology* (Toho Publishing)

"Gentlemen Callers" published in *Fractured Lit*

"How to Fail a Job Interview or Why You're the Only Wannabe Librarian Here" published in *Good River Review*

"How We Survive" published in *Lost Balloon*

"I Keep My Orgasms to Myself" published in *Surely Magazine*

"My Brother Scarecrow" published in *Apiary Magazine*

"One Last Pirouette" published in *Homology Lit*

"These Worn Bodies" published in *Flash Frontier*

"This Is a Story About a Fox" published in *Jellyfish Review*

'To All the Boys We Never Kissed" published in *South Florida Poetry Journal*

"Sausage People" published in *Homology Lit*

"So Many Clowns" published in *Five South Lit*

"Soba" published in *Black Warrior Review Online: The Fox Boyfriend Village*

"Something Between Them" published in *Cheap Pop*

"Sugar, Baby" published in *Five South Lit*

"Vagabond Mannequin" published in *Jellyfish Review*

"Your Husband Wants to be a Cardboard Cutout at the Last Blockbuster on Earth" published in *Bending Genres*

"White Ribbons" published in *Lost Balloon*

Moon City Press
Short Fiction Award Winners

2014
Cate McGowan
True Places Never Are

2015
Laura Hendrix Ezell
A Record of Our Debts

2016
Michelle Ross
There's So Much
They Haven't Told You

2017
Kim Magowan
Undoing

2018
Amanda Marbais
Claiming a Body

2019
Pablo Piñero Stillmann
Our Brains and the Brains
of Miniature Sharks

2020
Andrew Bertaina
One Person Away From You

2021
Michele Finn Johnson
Development Times Vary

2022
Lee Ann Roripaugh
Reveal Codes

2023
Avitus B. Carle
These Worn Bodies